Town Smokes

ABOUT THE AUTHOR

Pinckney Benedict, 23 years old, is the re-
cipient of two Transatlantic Review Awards
and the 1986 Nelson Algren Award. His
stories have appeared in the *Chicago Tribune*
and *Ontario Review*. A native of Lewisburg,
West Virginia, he is currently enrolled in
the graduate writing program at the University of Iowa.

TOWN SMOKES

stories by
Pinckney Benedict

Ontario Review Press / Princeton

Library of Congress Cataloging-in-Publication Data

Benedict, Pinckney, 1964–
Town smokes.

I. Title.
PS3552.E5398T68   1987   813'.54   87-5684
ISBN 0-86538-058-9 (pbk.)

"The Sutton Pie Safe" first appeared in the *Chicago
Tribune;* "Dog" and "Town Smokes" in the *Ontario Review.*

Cover photo by Chris Gachet
Design/typesetting by Backes Graphic Productions
Printed by Princeton University Press

Distributed by Persea Books, Inc.
225 Lafayette St., New York, NY 10012

For Cleve and Ann Benedict

Contents

The Sutton Pie Safe

A blacksnake lay stretched out on the cracked slab of concrete near the diesel tank. It kept still in a spot of sun. It had drawn clear membranes across its eyes, had puffed its glistening scales a little, soaking up the heat of the day. It must have been three feet long.

"There's one, dad," I said, pointing at it. My father was staring at the old pole barn, listening to the birds in the loft as they chattered and swooped from one sagging rafter to another. The pole barn was leaning hard to one side, the west wall buckling under. The next big summer storm would probably knock it down. The winter had been hard, the snows heavy, and the weight had snapped the ridge-pole. I wondered where we would put that summer's hay.

"Where is he?" my dad asked. He held the cut-down .410 in one hand, the short barrel cradled in the crook of his elbow, stock tight against his bare ribs. We were looking for copperheads to kill, but I thought maybe I could coax my dad into shooting the sleeping blacksnake. I loved the crack of the gun, the smell of sulphur from the opened breech. Again I pointed to the snake.

"Whew," he said, "that's a big one there. What do you figure, two, two and a half feet?" "Three," I said. "Three at least." He grunted.

"You gonna kill it?" I asked.

"Boys want to kill everything, don't they?" he said to me, grinning. Then, more seriously, "Not too good an idea to kill a blacksnake. They keep the mice down, the rats. Better than a cat, really, a good-sized blacksnake."

He stood, considering the unmoving snake, his lips pursed. He tapped the stock of the gun against his forearm. Behind us, past the line of willow trees near the house, I heard the crunch of gravel in the driveway. Somebody was driving up. We both turned to watch as the car stopped next to the smokehouse. It was a big car, Buick Riviera, and I could see that the metallic flake finish had taken a beating on the way up our lane.

My father started forward, then stopped. A woman got out of the car, a tall woman in a blue sun dress. She looked over the car at us, half waved. She had honey-colored hair that hung to her shoulders, and beautiful, well-muscled arms. Her wave was uncertain. When I looked at my dad, he seemed embarrassed to have been caught without a shirt. He raised the gun in a salute, decided that wasn't right, lowered the gun and waved his other hand instead.

It was too far to talk without shouting, so we didn't say anything, and neither did the woman. We all stood there a minute longer. Then I started over toward her.

"Boy," my dad said. I stopped. "Don't you want to get that snake?" he said.

"Thought it wasn't good to kill blacksnakes," I said. I gestured toward the house. "Who is she?" I asked.

"Friend of your mother's," he said. His eyes were on her. She had turned from us, was at the screen porch. I could see her talking through the mesh to my mother, nodding her head. She had a purse in her hand, waved it to emphasize something she was saying. "Your mom'll take care of her," my dad said. The woman opened the porch door, entered. The blue sun dress was pretty much backless, and I watched her go. Once she was on the porch, she was no more than a silhouette.

"Sure is pretty," I said to my father. "Yeah," he said. He snapped the .410's safety off, stepped over to the diesel pump. The snake sensed his coming, turned hooded eyes on him. The sensitive tongue flicked from the curved mouth, testing the air, the warm concrete. For just a second, I saw the pink inner lining of the mouth, saw the rows of tiny, backward curving fangs. "When I was ten, just about your age," my dad said, levelling the gun at the snake, "my daddy killed a big old blacksnake out in our back yard."

The snake, with reluctance, started to crawl from the spot of sun. My dad steadied the gun on it with both hands. It was a short weapon, the barrel and stock both cut down. It couldn't have measured more than twenty inches overall. Easy to carry, quick to use: perfect for snake. "He killed that blacksnake, pegged the skin out, and give it to me for a belt," my dad said. He closed one eye, squeezed the trigger.

The shot tore the head off the snake. At the sound, a couple of barn swallows flew from the haymow, streaked around the barn, swept back into the dark loft. I watched the body of the snake vibrate and twitch, watched it crawl rapidly away from the place where it had died. It moved more quickly than I'd seen it move that afternoon. The blood was dark, darker than beets or raspberry juice. My dad snapped the bolt of the gun open, and the spent cartridge bounced on the concrete. When the snake's body twisted toward me, I stepped away from it.

My dad picked the snake up from the mess of its head. The dead snake, long and heavy, threw a couple of coils over his wrist. He shook them off, shook the body of the snake out straight, let it hang down from his hand. It was longer than one of his legs. "Wore that belt for a lot of years," he said, and I noticed that my ears were ringing. It took me a second to understand what he was talking about. "Wore it 'til it fell apart." He offered the snake to me, but I didn't want to touch it. He laughed.

"Let's go show your mother," he said, walking past me toward the house. I thought of the woman in the sun dress, wondered what she would think of the blacksnake. I followed my dad, watching the snake. Its movements were slowing now, lapsing into a rhythmic twitching along the whole length of its body.

As we passed the smokehouse and the parked Riviera, I asked him, "What's her name?" He looked at the car, back at me. I could hear my mother's voice, and the voice of the other woman, couldn't hear what they were saying.

"Hanson," he said. "Mrs. Hanson. Judge Hanson's wife." Judge Hanson was a circuit court judge in the county seat; he'd talked at my school once, a big man wearing a three-piece suit, even though the day had been hot. It seemed to me that his wife must be a good deal younger than he was.

The snake in my father's hand was motionless now, hung straight down toward the earth. His fingers were smeared with gore, and a line of blood streaked his chest.

"Why'd you kill the blacksnake?" I asked him. "After what you said, about rats and all?" I was still surprised he'd done it. He looked at me, and for a moment I didn't think he was going to answer me.

He reached for the doorknob with his free hand, twisted

it. "Thought you'd know," he said. "My daddy made a belt for me. I'm gonna make one for you."

*   *   *

The woman in the sun dress, Mrs. Hanson, was talking to my mother when we entered the porch. "I was talking to Karen Spangler the other day," she said. My mother, sitting at the other end of the screen porch, nodded. Mrs. Spangler was one of our regular egg customers, came out about once every two weeks, just for a minute. Mrs. Hanson continued. "She says that you all have just the best eggs, and the Judge and I wondered if you might possibly . . ." She let the sentence trail off, turned to my father.

"Why, hello, Mr. Albright," she said. She saw the snake, but she had poise: she didn't react. My father nodded at her. "Mrs. Hanson," he said. He held the snake up for my mother to see. "Look here, Sara," he said. "Found this one sunning himself out near the diesel pump."

My mother stood. "You don't want to bring that thing on the porch, Jack," she said. She was a small woman, my mother, with quick movements, deft reactions. There was anger in her eyes.

"Thought I'd make a belt out of it for the boy," my dad said, ignoring her. He waved the snake, and a drop of blood fell from his hand to the floor. "You remember that old snakeskin belt I had?"

Mrs. Hanson came over to me, and I could smell her perfume. Her skin was tan, lightly freckled. "I don't think we've met," she said to me, like I was a man, and not just a boy. I tried to look her straight in the eye, found I couldn't. "No'm," I said. "Don't think we have."

"His name's Cates," my mother said. "He's ten." I didn't

like it that she answered for me. Mrs. Hanson nodded, held out her hand. "Pleased to meet you, Cates," she said. I took her hand, shook it, realized I probably wasn't supposed to shake a lady's hand. I pulled back, noticed the grime under my fingernails, the dust on the backs of my hands. "Pleased," I said, and Mrs. Hanson gave out a laugh that was like nothing I'd ever heard from a woman before, loud and happy.

"You've a fine boy there," she said to my dad. I bent my head. To my father, my mother said, "Why don't you take that snake out of here, Jack. And get a shirt on. We've got company."

He darted a look at her. Then he waved the snake in the air, to point out to everybody what a fine, big blacksnake it was. He opened the screen door, leaned out, and dropped the snake in a coiled heap next to the steps. It looked almost alive lying there, the sheen of the sun still on the dark scales. "Mrs. Hanson," he said, and went on into the house. He let the door slam behind him, and I could hear him as he climbed the stairs inside.

Once he was gone, Mrs. Hanson seemed to settle back, to become more businesslike. "The Judge and I certainly would appreciate the opportunity to buy some of your eggs." She sat down in one of the cane bottom chairs we kept on the porch in summer, set her purse down beside her. "But Sara—may I call you Sara?" she asked, and my mother nodded. "Something else has brought me here as well." My mother sat forward in her chair, interested to hear. I leaned forward too, and Mrs. Hanson shot a glance my way. I could tell she wasn't sure she wanted me there.

"Sara," she said, "you have a Sutton pie safe." She pointed across the porch, and at first I thought she meant the upright freezer that stood there. Then I saw she was pointing at the old breadbox.

My mother looked at it. "Well, it's a pie safe," she said. "Sutton, I don't know—"

"Oh, yes, it's a Sutton," Mrs. Hanson said. "Mrs. Spangler told me so, and I can tell she was right." Mrs. Spangler, so far as I knew, had never said anything to us about a pie safe. Mrs. Hanson rose, knelt in front of the thing, touched first one part of it and then another.

"Here, you see," she said, pointing to the lower right corner of one of the pie safe's doors. We'd always called it a breadbox, kept all kinds of things in it: canned goods, my dad's ammunition and his reloading kit, things that needed to be kept cool in winter. The pie safe was made of cherry wood—you could tell even through the paint— with a pair of doors on the front. The doors had tin panels, and there were designs punched in the tin, swirls and circles and I don't know what all. I looked at the place where she was pointing. "SS" I saw, stamped into the wood. The letters were mostly filled with paint; I'd never noticed them before.

Mrs. Hanson patted the thing, picked a chip of paint off it. My mother and I watched her. "Of course," Mrs. Hanson said, "this paint will have to come off. Oh, a complete refinishing job, I imagine. How lovely!" She sounded thrilled. She ran her hands down the tin, feeling the holes where the metal-punch had gone through.

"Damn," she said, and I was surprised to hear her curse. "What's the matter?" my mother asked. Mrs. Hanson looked closely at the tin on the front of the pie safe. "It's been reversed," she said. "The tin panels on the front, you see how the holes were punched in? It wasn't put together that way, you know. When they punched this design in the tin, they poked it through from the back to the front, so the points were outside the pie safe."

"Oh," my mother said, sounding deflated. It sounded

ridiculous to me. I couldn't figure why anyone would care which way the tin was put on the thing.

"Sometimes country people do that, reverse the tin panels," Mrs. Hanson said in a low voice, as if she weren't talking to country people. My mother didn't disagree. "Still, though," Mrs. Hanson said, "it is a Sutton, and I must have it. What will you take for it?"

I guess I should have known that she was angling to buy the thing all along, but still it surprised me. It surprised my mother too. "Take for it?" she said.

"Yes," Mrs. Hanson said, "it's our anniversary next week—mine and the Judge's—and I just know he would be thrilled with a Sutton piece. Especially one of the pie safes. Of course, I don't think it'll be possible to have it refinished by then, but he'll see the possibilities."

"I don't know," my mother said, and I couldn't believe she was considering the idea. "Is it worth a lot?" It was an odd way to arrive at a price, and I laughed. Both women looked at me as if they had forgotten that I was on the porch with them. I wondered what my father would say when he came down form putting on a shirt.

Mrs. Hanson turned back to my mother. "Oh, yes," she said. "Samuel Sutton was quite a workman, very famous throughout the Valley. People are vying to buy his pieces. And here I've found one all for myself. And the Judge." Then, as if understanding that she wasn't being wise, she said, "Of course, the damage to it, the tin and all, that does lower the value a great deal. And the paint." My father had painted the breadbox, the pie safe, when it had been in the kitchen years ago, to match the walls. We'd since moved it out to the porch, when my mother picked up a free-standing cupboard she liked better.

"I don't know," my mother said. "After all, we don't use it much anymore, just let it sit out here. And if you really want it . . ." She sounded worried. She knew my father wasn't going to be pleased with the idea. "We should wait, ask my husband." Mrs. Hanson reached into her handbag, looking for her checkbook. I knew it wasn't going to be that easy.

"Didn't that belong to Granddad?" I asked my mother. She looked at me, didn't answer. "Dad's dad?" I said, pressing.

"It was in my husband's family," my mother said to Mrs. Hanson. "He might not like it."

"Could we say, then, three hundred dollars? Would that be possible?" Mrs. Hanson asked. She wasn't going to give up. Just then, my father opened the door and stepped out of the house onto the porch. He had washed his hands, put on a blue chambray shirt, one I'd given him for Christmas.

"Three hundred dollars?" my father said. "Three hundred dollars for what?" I saw my mother's face set into hard lines; she was determined to oppose him.

"She wants to buy the pie safe," my mother said. Her voice was soft, but not afraid.

My father walked over to the breadbox, struck the tin with two fingers. "This?" he said. "You're going to pay three hundred for this?" Both my mother and Mrs. Hanson nodded. "I think that's a fair enough price, Mr. Albright," Mrs. Hanson said. I noticed she didn't call him Jack.

"You could use it to get someone over to help you work on the barn," my mother said. My father didn't even look at her. I moved to his side.

"Didn't know the breadbox was for sale," he said. "Didn't know that it would be worth that much if it was for sale."

"My father owned that," he said. "Bought it for my mother, for this house, when they were first married." He turned to my mother. "You know that," he said.

"But what do we use it for, Jack?" she asked. "We use the barn. We need the barn. More than some pie safe."

My father put his hand on my shoulder. "You're not going to leave me anything, are you?" he said to my mother. She flushed, gestured at Mrs. Hanson. Mrs. Hanson managed to look unflustered.

My dad looked at Mrs. Hanson. Her calm seemed to infuriate him. "We aren't merchants," he said. "And this isn't a furniture shop." He turned to me. "Is it, boy?" I nodded, then shook my head no, not sure which was the correct response. "Mrs. Hanson," my mother began. You could tell she didn't like my father talking like that to Mrs. Hanson, who was a guest in her home.

"Don't apologize for me, Sara," my dad said. "Go ahead and sell the damn breadbox if you want, but just don't apologize for me." My mother opened her mouth, shut it again.

"Boy," he said to me, "you want a snakeskin belt like I was talking about? Like my daddy made?" He gestured out the porch door, to where the headless snake lay. A big fly, colored like blue glass, was crawling on the body.

"Yes, sir," I said, glad not to have to look at the high color rising in Mrs. Hanson's cheeks.

"You come out back with me, then, and I'll show you how to skin it, how to stretch the hide. How'd that be?" Neither my mother nor Mrs. Hanson said a word. My dad pushed me ahead of him, and I headed out the door.

As he came after me, he turned and spoke through the screen. "I'll tell you something, Mrs. Hanson," he said. "You ought not to try to buy what hasn't been put up for sale."

*   *   *

Outside, my father groped in his pocket for a second, came up with his old Barlow knife, flicked the blade out. "You hold the snake for me," he said. "We'll take that skin right off him." He held out the body to me. I hesitated, reached out and took it.

It was heavy and rope-like, cool and limp in my hands. The scales were dry as sand. "Set it down there," my dad said, "and hold it stretched out tight." I set the snake down.

"Belly up," my dad said. "We don't want to mess up the scales on his back. That's what makes a snakeskin belt so nice, so shiny, them back scales." I rolled the snake. The scales on the sausage-like belly were light-colored, looked soft, and I prodded them with a forefinger. The skin rasped against my fingernail.

"Here we go," my father said, and pressed the blade of the knife against the belly of the snake. He always kept the knife razor-sharp, had a whetstone at the house he kept specially for it. I looked away. The knife made a sound as it went in; I thought I could hear him slicing through muscle, thought I could hear the small, cartilaginous ribs giving way under the blade.

Mrs. Hanson left the porch, and I could tell from the way she was walking that she must have gotten what she wanted. She moved with a bounce in her step. She looked over at us where we were kneeling, shook her hair back out of her face, smiled. My father paused in his cutting for a second when he heard the car door open. Mrs. Hanson backed the Buick around, headed back down the lane, toward the highway. A couple of low-hanging branches lashed the windshield as she went.

My mother stood on the porch, an outline behind the mesh of the screen, watching her go. When the car was out of sight, she turned and went back into the house.

My father gave a low laugh. When I looked at him, he was holding something gray between two fingers, dangled it back and forth in front of my face. "I'll be damned," he said. I looked down at the snake, the open stomach cavity, realized that he was holding a dead mouse by its tail. "No wonder that snake was so sleepy," my dad said. "He just ate." I stood, turned away from him.

"What's the matter?" he asked. I didn't answer. "You aren't gonna let that bother you," he said, and there was disdain in his voice. I put my arms over the top rail of the board fence around our yard, leaned my weight on it. I closed my eyes, saying nothing.

My father lowered his voice. "Thought you wanted that belt," he said. I wanted to turn to him, tell him that I did want the belt, just to give me a minute. I wasn't sure I could trust my voice not to break. "Guess not," he said.

Once again, I heard the sound of the knife, two quick cuts. I turned to look, saw that he had deftly sliced the body of the snake, had carved it into three nearly equal sections. It looked like pieces of bicycle tire lying there, bloody bicycle tire. My father rose, wiped his hands on his jeans.

"You think about that, boy," he said. "You think about that, next time you decide you want something." He walked past me, not toward the house, but toward the ruined barn.

Booze

The Duroc hog burst out of the brush not far from us, came out of the sinkhole, big and white and slat-ribbed, breathing hard. A few vines clung to its blunt snout. It paused at the edge of the field, blinking up at the bright, flat sky, its sides heaving like a bellows. It set off through the tall clover, grunting with each step.

Kenny and I were standing next to the post-hole digger, looking at an unfinished fence-post hole. The auger blade had caught a rock or a root about thirty inches down, leaving us with another twenty rods of fence to set and no way to do it. It looked to be a long job, getting that auger out of the ground. Then Kenny saw the hog.

"Booze!" he shouted. At first I didn't know what he meant. I watched the massive hog breasting through the grass. "Holy Christ," he said. "That's Booze."

I looked at the hog for a second longer, realized that he had to be right. "I bet it is," I said. It was thirty or forty yards from us, upwind, out of the brush, cutting a slanted path across the field. Even being that close to the bastard made me nervous. Booze was a rogue, a killer.

"Can you believe that?" Kenny said. "I figured he was dead." He leaned over and picked up the heavy-bladed brush hook which he used to clear bushes and small trees when we were setting fence. He looked like some kind of Viking standing there, strong and tan, almost wild, fingering the edge of his weapon. "Your dad still offering that fifty dollars?" he asked.

I blinked. "I guess so. Why?" I thought I knew. He lifted the brush hook in reply, flexed it in his big arms like a baseball bat, grinning. "Are you crazy?" I asked. I looked over at the hog's trail. Booze was moving slowly, all right, but the gap between us was widening all the time. He'd soon be into the windbreak at the edge of the south field, all scrub and undergrowth. It'd be impossible to take him in there. "You'll never get close to him," I said.

Kenny glared at me for a second, then began to move toward the hog at a trot. "You head him away from the brush, we'll split the fifty," he said over his shoulder. He knew I wasn't about to try, that I couldn't run fast enough to get there in time anyway. Besides, this wasn't going to be like herding cattle, just a wave and a shout. That hog was too damn big and too damn mean.

Kenny was head-down and sprinting, angling toward the place where the hog would enter the woods. He still moved like the vicious tackle he had been at Gilchrist High. He was big and fast, even with the brush hook in his hands, but I didn't think he'd get there in time to cut the hog off. If we'd still been in school—if it had been football season—I'd have bet he could do it. As it was, he was just wasting time. "No chance!" I yelled.

Unaware of us, Booze paused for a second to test the air, vine-covered snout up and flaring. He shifted his massive weight from leg to leg, his brittle hooves cracked and obviously sore. I saw the scoring along his humped back, a dozen black dots and pink hairless patches: my dad had blasted him with a shotgun on one of Booze's night raids years before. That was pretty much the last time anybody'd seen him.

Booze began to move again, straight ahead on his former path, heavy and slow, nearly six feet long. He was showing his age some, moving like an old man, favoring his left front leg. He was only yards from the windbreak.

Seeing Booze stop, Kenny put on a last burst of speed, cutting in front of the hog, stumbling for a second, foot caught in a thistle, then straightening. He stood, dripping sweat, bare chest heaving: his back to the trees, he clutched the heavy brush hook, swinging it loosely from his shoulders. His jaw was set, grim. I could see from his face that the size of the boar up close surprised him, scared him.

He braced as the big Duroc finally saw him; he brought the brush hook up, bare shoulders bunching with effort. Booze shrieked his anger at finding the path blocked, hauled himself forward, jaws open, making a kind of barking sound. Kenny had one shot, I realized, maybe not even one.

Leaning from the waist, throwing his good two hundred pounds behind it, Kenny brought the brush hook down.

*   *   *

"Hogs'll eat just about anything," Tobe Fogus had told me as he emptied the bucket into one of the feed troughs on the lot behind his house. The slop stank, stank like something dead. Skinny old Tobe fed his hogs garbage— banana peels, egg shells, any damn thing—because it was cheap. Like he said, they sure did eat it, and plenty of people were glad to let Tobe haul their trash. The hogs didn't know any better.

Tobe Fogus didn't smell too good himself. I tried to keep a little away from him, with his stained overalls and his spotted skin. He paid me fifty cents an hour to help him with the slopping and the rubdown in the afternoons. His place fronted ours on the east, so I made the walk across every day and stayed for a couple of hours. The jingle felt good in my pocket when I went home in the evenings, the extra dollar or so making my Quik-can bank heavier every night. I was twelve.

I emptied my slop bucket, shaking it like Tobe shook his to get the sticky gook off the bottom. I set it down and followed Tobe into the barn, where he kept the barrel of oil to rub the hogs down. He filled an old coffee can with used motor oil and handed it to me. "They'll eat anything," he said again. "But the big ones, the boars, they like meat."

I looked at him but said nothing. Tobe and I didn't converse much. Sometimes he talked, but he didn't particularly like me to answer. Most of the time I got the impression he wasn't talking to me anyway, that he would have gone on the same whether I was there or not. I lifted the can of oil and walked back out to the troughs, where the heavy, grunting hogs shouldered each other out of the way to get at the garbage.

They were a pale, sick-looking bunch, mainly Chester Whites. My dad, who raised dairy cattle and hated hogs anyway, especially despised Tobe's. "How's the disease crop, Eli?" he'd ask me when I came home in the evenings, black to the elbows with oil. Tobe used the oil on the hogs' hides to kill the fungus which always grew there. My dad told me the fungus was from the garbage Tobe fed his hogs and warned me that I'd catch it too if I didn't watch out.

I pushed one fat sow out of my way and knelt down among the hogs. The one I shoved never looked up; she just shoved the hog next to her over some, and so on down the line. I dipped a rag into the oil, hating the dirty feel of it on my hands, and began to work on her heaving, mottled back while she ate. The hogs were so intent on their slop that they never really noticed the oil bath. I rubbed the stuff onto the sow, working it in, as Tobe knelt down at another trough and started to do the same. "Elbow grease, remember," he said, looking at the hog next to him. I pressed harder on my sow and she grunted in annoyance.

Still to the hog, he said, "Yeah, they sure do like meat." He paused. "Your pa ever tell you what happened to Mrs. Fogus, boy? Ever wonder why I ain't got a wife?" he asked. I glanced up, but he wasn't looking at me. I had never particularly wondered; it was obvious to me that few women would want Tobe Fogus. I didn't say anything.

"Well, I'll tell you," he said. "The hogs et her." He chuckled. I finished up the sow and picked up my can, moving on to the next porker. I looked at her, probably a good three, four hundred pounds, ugly little eyes, short toothy snout. I looked at the rest, filling their mouths, chewing, swallowing the garbage, grunting and gurgling as they ate. I tried to imagine the whole bunch of them, lumpy and fungus covered, eating Mrs. Fogus. I imagined her to be thick and fat and repulsive, like them.

"Hogs wouldn't eat a person," I said finally. Tobe stopped oiling his sow for a second, then went on. I had made a mistake, contradicting him like that.

"You don't know nothing, boy," he said. I bent to my task, dipping the rag and wiping it on the bristling skin of the hog. "Ever see a big old boar hog go after a calf?" he asked. I didn't answer. "Hell, hog'll wait around a cow that's calving—snap up the calf, the afterbirth; eat up the whole ass end of the cow, you let it." I felt sick. "A person wouldn't be nothing, not to a big hog," he said.

Tobe Fogus chuckled again. "Yeah. Saw old Booze eat a bunch of chickens once. Just 'snap' and they were gone, feathers and all." Still I said nothing. He had forgotten that they hadn't been chickens, they had been guinea fowl, and they had been my mother's.

She had let them run loose in our yard and roost in our trees; they were her pets. One night, they crossed the short distance to Tobe Fogus' yard, roosted the night in his trees, set up their pecking and scratching in his yard the next morning. Several of them had gotten into Booze's pen. Booze had eaten them all, every last one. My mother cried and cried. It seemed silly to me to cry over guinea fowl.

Still, I felt myself flash angry for a moment, angry with old Tobe for not remembering that they hadn't been chickens. That was silly too. I set to work.

Booze was the only one of Tobe's hogs that wasn't infested with fungus. Tobe fed that hog the finest Purina hog chow with nutrients and additives year round. Booze had his own pen, surrounded by a four-rail board fence, with his own trough. The pen was big, probably two or three times the size Booze needed to stay healthy, but Tobe liked to see him run. I had to admit, Booze was worth the trouble and expense.

He was a full-grown Duroc boar hog, white-haired and huge, with the nastiest yellow eyes you ever saw; as different from those poor Chester sows as a hunting knife is from a spoon. His hide was flawless, shiny pink under stiff white bristles, stretched tight over bones and muscles and sinew. He was Tobe's breeding boar, probably the finest, strongest thing Tobe had ever owned. You could see how that old man swelled up when he looked at Booze, when he watched him go to rut on one of those sows, no match for his size, his weight, his immense strength and endurance. He was fierce and the sows always ended up winded and bitten. One poor bitch had even lost an ear to him.

Two tusks, larger than his other teeth, jutted out on either side of his broad lower jaw, the size of Havana cigars. Six feet long, more than five hundred pounds, nearer six hundred, with his hunched back and massive haunches, Booze was awesome and terrifying. Tobe could have rented him out for stud and made some good money, but he claimed that none of the dirt farmers around could pay enough for the likes of Booze. That was a serious decision for a man who had as little as Tobe Fogus did. There's not much money in hog farming.

"That Booze," Tobe said, moving on to another hog. "Like to put him up against a pit dog one day." Tobe was talking a lot. I winced to think about a dog in there with that monster. It would be a slaughter. A good-sized black bear, maybe; but Tobe wouldn't ever set Booze up where he might not win.

I finished up another sow, slapped her on her oily rump, and stepped away. I hardly even heard the grunting and squealing around me, I was so used to it. Tobe had just finished as well. He turned and faced me. "Hogs are good animals," he said. "And that Booze is the best. He can take care of himself." He reached out and took my can of oil from me. "That's one thing you got to learn in this world, boy. You got to learn to take care of yourself. Now get on home."

He fished a crumpled, greasy dollar bill out of one of his overall pockets and handed it to me, then turned back to the hog barn. I watched him for a second before I started out for home.

As I passed his pen on the way out, I saw old Booze

sitting back on his haunches, staring at me with his light, vicious eyes, looking between the second and third boards on his fence. He was chewing his mash, slowly and meditatively, chewing with a great deal of noise and relish. A string of saliva hung from his lower jaw to the ground. I went over the split-rail border fence, back onto our place, and on home.

*   *   *

I worked for Tobe Fogus for the rest of that summer, and off and on for the school year. I slopped and oiled his hogs, hosed them down and scraped up their manure. I helped to bury two of them that winter: they were sensitive to the cold, and the hog barn didn't offer much protection. It wasn't much more than a shed, really.

The hogs died of pneumonia and my mother was worried that I would get it too. I remember how those big, helpless hogs wheezed and snuffled as their lungs filled, how they lay on their sides looking half-squashed and dead already. Tobe didn't mourn his loss much. He just took special pains to make sure that Booze didn't get close to the dying ones, so that he would stay healthy. He rigged a tarp for the big boar out in his pen, with loads of fresh straw. He led an extension cord from the kitchen of the house so he could put a hundred-watt bulb under the tarp. Booze stayed warm that winter.

Next spring, Tobe hired Kenny Yates from the other side of our farm to help me with the hogs. Kenny and I had been friends since before grade school, and I was glad to have the help. Tobe was pretty old and he hadn't stood the winter well. He didn't work with the hogs so much anymore. Now that he had Kenny, he left most of that up to us.

Booze was his especial care; we weren't allowed to fool with him. "Too vicious," Tobe Fogus said. "Too vicious for you boys by half." He mixed Booze's mash for him, slopped it into the trough, talking to the hog all the while. "Eat it, hog bastard," he'd say. "Snap it up you monster son of a bitch."

Sometimes he would come out to where Kenny and I were rubbing the sows down and stare at them, reminding us how important elbow grease was. One day, I remember, in early June of that summer, he came out when Kenny and I were finished and handed each of us a dollar bill and two quarters. "A raise," he said, not very loud, and went back inside, weaving a little, like a drunk man. He'd been like that for a while, kind of pained around the eyes. We were glad of the extra quarter an hour, Kenny and I were, and neither of us worried particularly about Tobe Fogus. Nobody much did.

* * *

It was early in the next fall that he died, just after Labor Day. Kenny and I had finished school for the day—it was a Thursday—and we came to the split-rail fence which marked the boundary between our land and Tobe Fogus'. Kenny had to tell Tobe that he couldn't come by every day anymore. He was going to have to start spending time in football practice at the junior high. He was a rising tackle, almost sure to make first string his eighth-grade year, if he worked at it.

As we came across, we saw that the fence was missing two rails out of the bottom of one section. They lay a couple of yards away and one of them was broken in the center. We propped them up as best we could. Kenny straightened and glanced around the hog yard, then grabbed my arm.

"Booze's pen," he said. One section of fence was broken, the boards ripped from the posts. Booze was gone.

Kenny looked around. "You don't figure he's still around here some place, do you?" he asked. I thought that the broken rails where we'd come through the fence meant that he wasn't, that he was on our place now, but you could never tell. I didn't want to face Booze without a good stout barrier between us. I thought about those yellow, crooked tusks.

"Mr. Fogus!" Kenny called toward the house. "Hey, Tobe!" He lowered his voice on the second yell, glancing around. He was big, firming up even then, but he didn't exactly anticipate having six hundred pounds of mean hog down on top of him either. "You figure he knows the hog is gone?" he asked me. We started walking toward the house. I figured Tobe would know what to do. He could face Booze. "I don't know," I said. "Guess we'd better tell him."

"Mr. Fogus!" Kenny yelled again but it didn't come out very loud. "You there?" We stood on the porch. It was a cool afternoon but only the screen door was closed. On the porch, we felt safer. We could run into the house if we had to.

Inside, the tv was on. A sow grunted at the trough behind us, wanting dinner. I knocked. "Mr. Fogus," I said. "Anybody home?" He didn't answer.

Kenny moved in front of me. He rapped the door hard and called out. "Booze is gone, Mr. Fogus. Booze got out." We listened but all we could hear was the tv in the parlor just off the front hall. If he was in there, he should have been able to hear us. The tv wasn't that loud.

Kenny pulled the door open a little. "Should we go in?" he asked. I nodded, so he slipped the rest of the way inside, with me behind him. Neither of us had been inside the house before, not beyond the front hall. Tobe had never asked us. The house looked and smelled like him— his overalls hung from a hook by the door, two pairs of them, along with his dark green wool hat. There was a telephone on a small, rickety phone table, a party line which he hardly ever used. Next to that was a roll-top desk, open and full of paper, batteries, all manner of junk.

Kenny tried again. "Mr. Fogus?" Still no answer. He knocked lightly on the parlor door, then pushed it open. The tv was on, an old RCA black-and-white on a rolling stand, and Tobe Fogus sat in front of it, tv dinner laid out before him. His head lay on the frayed lace doily spread over the back of the recliner, jaw slack, eyes closed.

*   *   *

Afterwards, my mother and father and I sat around the dinner table, talking the whole thing over. I think it shook my mother up more than anybody, even me, though I had found the body. "It's awful," she said, "dead with his food in front of him like that." Tobe had just taken a bite of Salisbury steak when he died, hadn't even had time to swallow. It seemed like a strange thing for her to dwell on. Food or no food, Tobe Fogus was still dead, and Booze was still gone. Nobody seemed to attach a whole lot of importance to the hog. Nobody but me and Kenny.

"Kenny says Tobe knew he was going to die," I told my father. "He says Tobe let Booze loose before his lights went out."

"Before his lights went out," my dad said. "That's not very respectful." He didn't seem to mind the disrespect much. "I doubt that's the way it happened," he said. "You ask Kenny why Tobe would bust the boards up like that, a dying man, when he could just have opened the gate."

I didn't have an answer for that. "I'll tell you what I think happened," he continued. "I think Tobe died in the evening, early, without having fed the old boar yet. Along about the morning, Booze got so hungry he couldn't wait anymore. He went out after some food. Sound good to you?"

I nodded. "So what are you going to do?" I asked. My dad looked at me. "About Booze," I added.

"I hadn't thought about it," he said. Then he smiled. "Tell you what. I'll give fifty dollars to the man who brings the wild white hog in."

"Dead or alive?" I asked.

"A hog?" my dad said. "Dead."

* * *

Tobe's sows were packed into a truck and shipped off, sold for a pitifully small price. Nobody knew where Booze was. Negotiations began among the lawyers about what to do with the land. My dad made a bid for it to extend our boundaries to the east, but he lost. Some professional guy bought it, a gentleman farmer, and moved in a herd of big gray Simmentals. My father disliked them almost as much as he had the hogs. "Useless doctor's cattle," he said. "Just a damn tax shelter."

Fifty dollars was a lot of money as far as Kenny and I were concerned. Every afternoon when we had the time we would set off with our .22s, my Savage pump and Kenny's Winchester semiauto, scouring the fields and sinkholes for the big boar. We found traces of him from time to time—hog trails, broken branches, droppings—but we didn't see Booze himself. From fall until midwinter, we spent at least one evening a week looking for Booze.

I don't know what we would have done if we had found

him. Our little rimfire rifles would hardly have punched through his hide, let alone killed him. Kenny claimed that he was going to shoot for the eyes. If one of the eye shots brought him down, Kenny said, he got the whole fifty dollars. I didn't argue.

When the snow started to pile up and we had to use snowshoes to get around in the fields, it got to seem less like fun and more like work lugging rifles all around. The fifty dollars lost its reality for us, was forgotten by everybody else. Dad had known I would never find Booze, had known he would never have to pay the bounty. There was nothing I could do about it. No matter how hard Kenny and I looked, no matter how many hours spent waiting at the edges of sinkholes, how many evenings spent quiet and freezing in the fields, we never so much as saw the hog. After a while we stopped trying completely. I began to doubt that Booze was even on our land, had been at all.

Later in the winter, though, not long after Kenny and I stopped hunting him, Booze turned up, turned up vicious. There is nothing worse or more dangerous than a rogue boar, especially a Duroc as big as Booze.

It started with the rabbits. For years my family had kept rabbits in a wire hutch behind the house. At the moment there were three white females and one big black chinchilla buck. We called them meat rabbits—had even tried to start a cottage industry breeding them for meat—but after selling off the first lot we couldn't bear to do it anymore. We just kept them back there, fat and happy, and gave the babies away to people who wouldn't eat them.

One day I went to feed the rabbits and found that the wire mesh on one side of the cage had been pushed in, bent and ruptured. Inside the hutch, there was fur and blood on the trampled snow, nothing else. My dad found prints, a hog's cloven hooves, and said that Booze had done it. He raged about the problem that old Tobe Fogus had left him, talking about the damage a hog like Booze could do if it wanted. I understood that he had never, up to that moment, believed that Booze was on the place. He still saw it as just an inconvenience, a potential livestock problem. I was scared. That night, for the first time, I dreamed about Tobe, jaws open and full of uneaten food.

Tuesday of the following week, Kenny's father Calvin came across the farm to talk with my dad. He was a big man, half a head taller than my father. He looked angry. "Something has got to be done, Pierce," he said. "That thing came again last night. Right into the coop, right through the chicken screen. Took two of my best layers." He grimaced, stood up from the chair he'd been sitting on, grasped the back in his strong hands. "I could live with that, Pierce. But it got Tippy." I winced. Tippy had been Kenny's dog, a scrappy little border collie.

"Tippy went out there when he heard the chickens. By the time I got on a pair of jeans and grabbed the gun, that son of a bitch was out of there. Just feathers everywhere—" He swallowed. "—and Tippy. For God's sake, Pierce, that hog killed a full-grown dog. We'll soon have lambs out there, and the sheep . . ."

"Already got one of the sheep," my father said. It was the first I'd heard about it. I pictured Booze, huge and bristling, slaughtering a sheep, empty-headed and too scared to run.

"That much the more, then," Cal Yates said. "I say we go out after him. I'll be damned if I lose any more livestock to some hog."

"Rogue boar," my dad said. "The worst kind." He rose and got his coat. "Get me my rifle, Eli," he said. I paused. "The Remmy," he said.

I knew he couldn't miss with the Remington. It was a

sweet 7-millimeter magnum, a real stopper. Dad had gone all out and bought a Weatherby 6-to-60 scope for it. He didn't used it often, but when he did, he was good. I took him the rifle and a box of shells. He snapped three into the magazine, then handed the rest back to me. "Takes more than three with this rifle, that hog deserves to get away," he said.

He headed out the door, following Cal. They walked across the porch and out to Cal's Scout, where his lever-action 30-30 lay snug in the gun rack. Dad whistled and clapped his hands: Music and Homer, our two bear dogs, jumped into the back of the truck, anxious for the hunt. Dad and Cal climbed in and the hunting party headed into the fields.

My dad didn't get back until that evening after the sun had gone down. When he walked in, looking cold and deeply tired, I knew he hadn't gotten the hog. "I'm getting too old," he told my mother. He turned to me, put a hand on my shoulder. "We lost Homer, boy," he said. He looked terrible, uncertain; I was afraid he might cry. He laid the Remmy down on the kitchen table, bolt open, and went upstairs. I felt tears come to my eyes: for Homer, killed in the snow by a rogue boar. I fought them back.

I snapped the clip out of the rifle. It was empty. My father had fired three rounds at the bastard and Booze had still managed to get the dog. Three rounds. This time I couldn't hold the tears.

*   *   *

For a long time after that, it seemed like Booze was always with us, never far enough away to be forgotten. My dad had emptied the Remmy and lost his best dog— had given up. He didn't seem to want to try anymore. At

night I often fell asleep thinking about the quarter ton of
killer hog which lived in some sinkhole probably not too
far away.

When spring came, Booze showed just how bad he could
be. One calf, two, then three—a half dozen altogether
during that first year. Calvin took to staying up nights,
30-30 cradled in his arms, straining to see, to hear the hog.
Kenny and I sat up with him more than once, drinking
coffee and looking for the white shape of Booze to drift
into our sights. He never did.

One night in August of that year I dreamed about Tobe
and about Booze. Somehow they were all mixed up together. Tobe was dead, sitting in his recliner; and then he
wasn't, smiling with a hog's face, ugly yellow tusks, grunting. It scared me so bad I woke up.

Woke up and listened, the spit leaving my mouth, leaving it dry. Our lone old bluetick, Music, started sounding,
high and loud. Below my window, something big grunted.
Booze was in the trash cans. One of them crashed over
and I could smell the garbage, hear the hog, chewing and
swallowing. I sat stock-still in bed, wondering if anyone
else had heard the noise. The hog knocked over another
trash can.

From the porch, Dad let go with one barrel of his Brown-
ing 12-gauge. Booze screamed. I smelled the powder,
heard the rest of the cans go down, rolling and clattering
as the hog thrashed and fought. My dad fired the second
barrel and I heard the pellets hit the cans like gravel slung
at a tin roof. Booze screamed again and was gone, in what
direction I couldn't tell. "Scorched you, you bastard!" my
dad yelled from the porch. I heard the screen door slam
as he came back inside. A moment later he was at my
bedroom door in his boxer shorts, shotgun still gripped in
his right hand.

"Scorched him, Eli," he said.
"Sure did, Dad," I said.
"Go to sleep. He won't be back."
"Yes sir."
"Go to sleep."
Outside, Music started to quiet down. Somewhere Booze was sitting alone in the brush and August heat, biting at pellets too deep to work loose. I wished him pain, wished that he would die.

* * *

After that night, the night my dad shot him, nobody saw much of Booze. We didn't know for sure whether he was alive or not. From then on people took extra care with their children on the place. Kenny and I didn't go camping out in the fields that summer like we had always done. I never really felt good out on the farm without my deer rifle. The farm seemed changed somehow, a place where a monster had lived. Of course, I couldn't say that to anyone.

I went through junior high, high school, and only saw Booze once in all that time. I saw him while I was raking hay up along the eastern fence line, near what had been Tobe's place years before.

He was in the brush, a big white blur, moving slowly, keeping pace with the tractor. Following the row of drying hay, I lost sight of him. By the time I came around again, he was gone. I remember how relieved I felt.

Kenny hadn't seen him at all, claimed to be sure he was dead, claimed that my dad had managed to kill him that night. "It's like Bigfoot," he said. "People aren't sure what they see, so they call it Bigfoot. You call it Booze." We had nearly gotten into a fight over that one. He dropped a full nelson on me, though, and shut me down before I could get too mad.

Calves disappeared, sure, but a few calves are bound to on a place as big as ours was. If the number was a little higher than usual, it seemed like nobody really wanted to figure it out. It was easier to believe that Booze was dead.

*   *   *

It was a killing blow, well aimed. The thick, curved blade of the brush hook caught the boar hard between the eyes, knocked him to his knees. The blade hooked in bone for a second and Kenny stumbled forward, actually pushed himself off the boar's shoulder to stand. He swung the brush hook up to strike again.

In that moment between Kenny's first blow and the one to follow, Booze snapped blindly sideways and caught one of Kenny's ankles. Yanked off balance, Kenny hit Booze again, on the side of the neck. The blade sank deep into the loose flesh and stuck there, the wooden handle jerked from Kenny's hands. Kenny was down, and I could see his mouth moving; I couldn't hear his voice.

Booze dragged himself forward. Kenny jerked his ankle free, backed away, sliding, using his good leg and his elbows, weaponless. The white hog drooled blood, choking.

I shrieked at Kenny to get up, get up. I started to run toward him as hard as I could, empty-handed. Kenny stared in horror. I thought I was going to be sick. Split from snout to ears, grunting, Booze came on, stumbling, catching himself. His rear legs quivered. He should have been dead.

As the boar reached Kenny, thrust his snout down, searching for something to bite, to crush, his hind legs collapsed: slowly, slowly. His jaws worked, closed on a pants leg, closed almost gently on Kenny's sneaker. Kenny snatched his leg back. Booze shoved himself forward again. Blood soaked the grass, spattered Kenny.

Then I was there, kicking the boar hard, feeling the toe of my boot smack against his ribs. I could feel the heat coming off him, hear his grunts, bubbling wheezes. He smelled like rotten pork.

His head came around, grotesque and awful. A single yellow eye peered dully at me. I knew he was going to kill me; there was nothing I could do.

With a groan, a hot rush of air, Booze rolled to one side, away from me, muscles jerking. His jaw clamped shut, then open, shut again. His hooves, surprisingly small and delicate on such a monster hog, drummed against the ground. His blunt snout, the size of a man's work boot, thumped to the ground, teeth bared. Still his rib cage rose and fell, slower and slower.

"Help me, for Christ's sake!" Kenny yelled. His leg was caught underneath the hog, his lips drawn tight, face pale with pain and shock. Booze shifted again, blinded, dying, but still powerful. I couldn't make myself get close to where he lay.

Kenny was scrabbling at the grass, pulling up handfuls of it, trying to work himself loose. I managed to go to him, to get a hold on his shoulders. He was slippery with blood. A hog like that, I knew, must have gallons of blood. It was impossible to tell how much of it was Kenny's. His leg was a mess. He looked at it briefly, looked away again. I didn't know what to do. Booze was down, dead.

"Son of a bitch," Kenny said, gritting his teeth. "Son of a bitch is done for." Booze shuddered and the whistle of his breath began to die away. The handle of the brush hook stood straight up from his neck, trembling.

I put an arm around Kenny to help him up, get him over to the tractor. "Son of a bitch got me. But I got him, didn't I?" he said. He really seemed to want an answer. I thought he was delirious. My knees felt weak.

I looked over at Booze, the size of a young bull, not all the way dead yet. The sour smells of blood and animal piss reached me, the ripe odor of hog manure. Booze's muscles had started to relax. I leaned against the tractor.

His corpse was bigger than any boar's had a right to be, huge and white there in the green clover. I knew it was going to take a hell of a chain or steel cable to drag Booze out of the field. I could picture it, the great hog with the chain around his back legs, dragged across the pastures to the pit where we put the dead cattle. It was going to be quite a job to roll the dead hog down into the pit but I figured we would manage it.

All The Dead

Adonijah Adonijah you got to get up my mama says. I pull the covers up some but she is tuggen at me and it is hard to ignore.

Jesus mama I say. I know that it ain' time to get up just yet. It is dark outside.

Your daddy is gone she says and her hand clutches my shoulder hard. I can feel the bones of her fingers and the metal of the rings on her hand. I see that she ain' wearen nothen but her nightdress and that is unusual in front of the kids.

My daddy been gone a long time I say.

She steps back and her mouth is open. She is a pretty woman in the mornen dark with the long gold hair loose down her back. She generally pins it up tight against her head so that it don' get in the way. With it down it is not so easy to see the age setten on her like a crow on a fence post.

Makepeace you mean I say. Makepeace gone off in the middle of the night.

The other kids—Byron and Ben—they're awake over

in their bed and I know they are listenen. They are Makepeace's boys and call him daddy. Mama walks out the room and I know she is ready to bawl. They ain' nothen worse then maken your mama cry. I reach down off the bed, stretch around with my hand looken for my jeans that I dropped the night before.

I heard him go out Ben says and I can see his eyes over next the wall. He's setten up in the bed. He was God-a-mighty pissed Ben says.

You hush and get back asleep I say. I can hear my mama out in the front room moven around and I think she may be getten dressed ready to go out after Makepeace. I pull on my jeans and shove into my boots.

He ain' want you to come after him Byron says and the two of them are setten there in the dark staren at me. They are young and of course never known my daddy. I didn' know him all that good myse'f, when he died. That was ten year ago, before Makepeace come around at all.

I couldn' care less what it is that Makepeace wants but I don' say nothen to them. I buckle my belt and head out into the front room. I pull the door to behind me. My eyes feel sticky and hot with sleep dirt.

Curtis is a good man my mama says. Better then you know she says.

I don' say nothen back.

He is my husband and the father of them boys in there she says. Don' that mean nothen to you?

I say I'm up ain' I.

My hands are stiff and scabbed with wrestlen the beef onto the hooks down to the slaughterhouse so I chafe them together, try to work some heat into them. I know Jeffries, the fellow that owns the place, got a couple dozen market hogs comen in the mornen. Hogs is the worst because they scream and jump when you cut them and spout the hot blood everwhere.

Makepeace works down there too. It was him that got me the job though I sure as hell don' like to say it. He's foreman on the shift and all the time yellen at me. I hold my end up but seem like don' nothen keep him happy.

He gone up to Doolittle's my mama says. Took the truck 'bout twenny minutes ago. Doolittle owes him some money.

He been drinken I say.

She nods at me. Took the pistol she says.

Christ have mercy I say.

Echols Doolittle is a bootlegger that lives up in the hollers a couple miles beyond us, up on Tree Mountain. He is all the time haven to go up to the farm at Huttonsville to do short stretches. I hear tell some guys call him Iron Eyes 'cause he got no light of the soul in his face when he looks at you but is just blank and cold as river ice.

I figure Makepeace must of sold him some potatoes off the back plot for the muddy liquor Doolittle is all the time maken. I know that Doolittle ain' the man to mess with at a quarter of three in the mornen.

Here's your coat she says and holds out the big sheep-skin jacket to me. It smells like slaughterhouse meat when I pull it on and turns my stomach over. It's cool out she says.

You bet I say.

The old Mercury my mama used to drive sets in the yard like a giant dog that is sleepen, settled down on four flats. She ran it without water a couple summers back and fried the head-gasket. Makepeace swore it'd set there till it rotted and that is just what it has done. Squirrels live in next the engine block in summer, and they use the insulation off the hood to make nests with. My mama has planted tall flowers around it in a kind of bed. I have never knew whether she meant it as a joke or just thought it would make the rusted junker look better. Of course it is October now and the flowers are nothen but dead yellow stalks anyway.

My mama stands on the porch as I head out for Doolittle's. It ain' much more then thirty degrees and I can see her breath risen in the circle of light from the porch lamp. I figure she will leave that light on till I get home with Makepeace. I jerk the collar of the jacket up around my ears, get used to the blood smell. It is funny that I don' ever notice it when I wear the jacket in the day.

*   *   *

A state trooper name of J.W. Daws shot my daddy in the face with his Colt .38 Special and killed him dead as hell. A black boy pulled a gun in a Seven-Eleven down in Yarbro just about the time my daddy was goen in for a cup of coffee one mornen. The trooper was parked acrost Route 60 in a plain brown state car and seen the whole thing as it come down.

When he come in the store with his gun pulled, the black boy let go and the trooper returned fire and I guess my daddy didn' get down out the way. From what I hear he was a good-looken man before he got shot but mebbe not too good when it come to thinken quick. He worked down to the Firestone plant and after his death was very sore missed as I understand it.

I have met J.W. Daws and I know he is very sorry about the shooten. He is in his middle thirties and not with the state boys anymore but a builden contractor in one of the neighbor counties, Pocahontas or Monroe, I can' remember which. He is a dark-haired man with a beefy middle and very well-spoke.

He come to the funeral which must of took more guts than many a man has. He stood next to my mama and give her his handkerchief when she started in to cry. He looked very fine and stern in his dress trooper uniform and round hat, looken down at the grave when they planted my daddy. The state bought the box they put him in. I don' recall what happened to the black boy: Daws didn' quite kill him and I figure he must of gone to Moundsville for a time, though likely as not he is out now or mebbe back in on some other charge.

*   *   *

It takes me the better part of an hour to hike up the side of Tree to where Echols Doolittle got his place. I am all sweated up by the time I get there and it seems like the sky is getten lighter colored to the east. That is the false dawn that they talk about and the sun will not really rise for another two hour or more. Some winter birds are fooled and I can hear them starten the day in the branches over my head.

Doolittle's place is back in a holler where the ground is all marl and swamp and the grass is thick and grabs at your pant leg. It smells like somebody been spreaden lime. The ground is pitted and uneven in places. An old yellow dog watches me from the edge of the woods. His black wet lips curl back and I see that his teeth are brown and ground flat with age.

There is light in the windows I am surprised to see at this hour. The light is blue and flickers, light from the tv screen. It is an old double-wide trailer that Doolittle lives in and I figure it must of been a bitch to get it up the moun-

tain. I know Doolittle got a generator 'cause the power
lines sure as hell don' get up in there. I listen and I can
make out the sound of the two-cylinder diesel bangen away
somewhere out the back.

Strung all along one side of the trailer they is a mess of
snakeskins, look like diamondback and some of them four
foot long and better. The skins is shriveled and bunched
like the skin of an old woman's fingers.

A body moves in one of the windows so I know they
are about. Yo the house I call and my voice sounds terrible
loud in the holler. I don' want to shout again so I walk to
the trailer. I look around but Makepeace's truck ain' in the
yard. There is just some old Pontiac Catalina that somebody lift-kitted the rear end and put wide tires and Cragar
alloy rims on. A little Suzuki dirt bike, no more then a
hunnerd cc and covered with dry red mud, is leanen
against the Catalina. It occurs to me Doolittle's stills must
be a good way up the mountain and he mebbe needs the
bike to get up there to them. It is my idea to leave but I
got to find out about Makepeace.

Doolittle smacks the door open. It is a light door and
bangs hard against the tin side of the trailer. Who is it he
shouts and I know he can' see me very well in the dark.
I lean against the Pontiac and the shocks don' give at all.
It is set up stiff like that for a good solid ride goen fast.
Out in front of the trailer Doolittle got a little low four-
legged steel table for target shooten and sighten scopes
in. The table got an oarlock bolted to it to rest the rifle on.

Doolittle ain' very tall but wide as an ax-handle acrost
the shoulders and got a deer rifle tucked under one arm.
He got an old leather US cavalry holster strapped on his
waist. The leather of the holster is black with age and use
and he's cut the bottom off so he can fit in a long-barreled
automatic pistol, what they call a Bolo Mauser.

He got no shirt on but just a pair of jeans that the fly ain' even all the way up. I can' figure how he stands the cold. He's looken at me and blinken while he gets used to the dark.

They is talk that Doolittle is liven up here with his cousin as his wife but I figure that is just trash talken. People are all the time sayen that kind of thing but seldom is it ever true.

Looken for Curtis Makepeace I say.

What is it makes you think he is here Doolittle says.

He has got me found in the dark now but he don' bring the rifle around or nothen. I am a tall skinny kid and I guess don' look like much in the way of a threat to some-body like Doolittle.

He tole my mama he's comen up I say.

And she wanted you to come and get the son a bitch Doolittle says. He laughs and props the rifle against the door jamb behind him, walks out into the yard. His feet are bare and sink down in the swampy ground. I figure he is bound to catch pneumonia.

When he gets close to me I can smell the liquor on him. I don' know whether it is what he's put down himse'f or what he's made. Mebbe the smell of it is on him the way the slaughterhouse stink is on my jacket. He zips himse'f the rest of the way down and pisses against a tire on the Pontiac. The piss steams is how cold it is. Doolittle's big meaty face lights up while he goes.

After a while he closes his pants, leans against the car next to me.

You like the car do you he says. I don' say nothen. I see what they mean about his eyes. They are gray and flat as stones.

You know what we do up here Doolittle says and he ain' smilen anymore.

I ain' know nothen I say.

He grabs a fistful of my hair and pulls me toward him. He shakes me back and forth by the hank of hair and tears come to my eyes. I want to close them but don'. I look him in the face as much as I can that close up, big and white as the full moon.

You goddam right he says and he don' make his voice very loud at all. You goddam right you don' know nothen, come up here and yell at people's houses he says.

He lets go my hair and I rub the spot, try to take some of the fire out of it. In a fight I know Doolittle got to take me apart. He's got a good thirty pounds on me and he's not very old, mebbe forty. Beside, he's got that iron strapped on his waist. He's grinnen again and I see he is crazy, nuts as a monkey liven up there in the holler.

Makepeace figures I owe him Doolittle says. I tole him he might just as well forget it. Them taters was small and black as coal with the crud. He knows better then Echols Doolittle gon' pay for some rotted spuds.

You know where he went I say.

I can' be too careful he says. I got people wanten to kill me you know.

No I didn' know I say.

Makepeace brung a piece with him when he come Doolittle says. He was drunk and argumentative and put a hole in the trailer.

I feel cold, knowen now what has prob'ly conspired with Makepeace up here in the holler. That Mauser could knock a chunk off of a man and the same for the rifle in the door. I will mebbe not walk away from this place and my knees go soft on me. It is good that I am leanen against the Catalina.

Where is he at I say. Off in the woods a great horn owl

gives out with its call, like some kind of a bronze bell out there.

Doolittle spreads his arms like he is taken in the whole Tree Mountain above us, the woods and the hollers and the shale cliffs of it. It is like he didn' hear me at all.

They's a number of dead men up in there he says. A powerful number.

You kill them I say. Doolittle is stone out of his mind and his face is calm as he says all this. His lips are a little blue with the cold. I don' know what to believe or not. It makes me shiver to think about.

A couple he says. And other men. The mountain done some of them too. Don' get the idee that it was only me.

Jesus Doolittle a woman yells from the door of the trailer. She is good-looken standen there in just a man's shirt and a pair of underpants, huggen herse'f from the cold. Her hair is short and dark and standen up like she been asleep.

Get your ass in out the cold she says.

Doolittle stirs off the car, steps toward her.

Did you kill him I say to his back. My voice shakes because I am scared.

The woman in the door hears me. He didn' kill nobody she says. Though there was one that just about begged for it.

Doolittle shouts at her Shut you up Polly Boo.

He gone in town that son a bitch Makepeace I would bet says the woman Polly Boo from the door. Or mebbe he gone home.

Doolittle brushes past her and I am glad to see him inside. I wonder is it safe to run out of the holler and away from these two. Polly Boo pulls the door shut.

Up high next the doorjamb I can see a hole that I figure Makepeace might of put there with the .45 pistol that he brought up with him. It is a hole the size of a half dollar and it looks like they got a rag or somethen stuffed in it to keep the cold out.

Further off then the time before, the horn owl calls again. It is a lonesome sound from up there on the mountain, sound like a man that has died callen out, for what ain' nobody knows.

*   *   *

When I was ten year old, Monkey Granger beat the bejesus out of me up at the limestone quarry. It is one of them things that kids are getten themse'f into all the time. Me and Monkey was pals, really, but I was maken fun of the way he walked, all hunched over and them long arms down and like to drag the ground. That was why we called him Monkey but all the other times he never seemed to of minded it. He was a big boy and older, haven failed a couple time, and seem like he was all the time grinnen and putten up with it.

I remember I'm standen at the edge of the quarry pond and the water is chill and deep and dark as coal oil. Monkey's standen there with me and he still got all his clothes on. It's June, just the first part of vacation, and we're all stripped off for swimmen, pushen each other in the water and yellen.

A couple of the older kids is tossen pennies in the deep part and goen off the ledges after them. They been told not to do that because some boy not too long before cracked his skull on the bottom and busted his neck, but wasn' nobody gon' to pay any attention. We used to talk about that boy when we camped out and wanted to scare each other at night, about what it's like to be thirteen year old and be dead and cold and floaten in the quarry water.

Monkey I say to him you got to strip off if you goen in.

He just looks at me and grins a little but it ain' much of a grin.

Figure I'll set this one out he says and flops down on the side of the pond, don' even stick his feet in. He's a big boy like I say and his feet stick out real clumsy in his old tore-up Keds. Right away I figure what's up with him.

You afraid to get in the water I say.

He don' say nothen and I know that's what it is. Monkey don' want to get in the water 'cause he's scared. I wonder what the hell he come with us for, mebbe thought the courage would come over him when he got to the quarry with the rest of us.

That's prett' funny I say. I guess that's just all right for a Monkey to be scared of the water.

Some of the other kids are comen around us and Monkey's getten uncomfortable about it all. You want to hush up Adonijah he says but I don' have the sense.

This here Monkey's scared to go in the water I'm yellen, and he can tell it's gon' be in their mind prett' soon to toss him in. He don' want that and he's up on his feet, comen over to me, tryen to put a hand on my mouth.

Shut the hell up he says.

We got a scared Monkey here I call out and I can hear the other boys picken up the call around the quarry. Monkey's shiften from one foot to the other and I bend over, scrape my knuckles on the ground, make hooten noises through my lips. I scratch at my armpits just like a chimp and it's the funniest damn thing I ever did. Everbody's laughen like hell and ready to give old Monkey the dunk of his life.

Then he hits me and I swear to God he like to take my head off. I go down and he's all over me, arms and elbows and knees and shouten No sir No sir No sir over and over again. I never did know what he was yellen that for. He sticks a hard fist in my eye and busts my lips and bloodies my nose, hits me in the throat so I can' stop coughen. It's a hell of a thing and we're both cryen to bust a gut.

It don' take but a couple minutes for Monkey to rack me up real good and then he's gone, headen out the quarry and through the scrub brush till he gets back home. Next thing they ain' nobody at the quarry but me. All the others just lit out when they seen Monkey take off on me.

I'm layen there and tasten what my blood tastes like and blowen it out my nose in long strings, wipen it onto the rocks I'm layen on. It's hard to believe how beautiful the color is when it's all new and just out of you like that, beaden up on the limestone. Everthen feels kind of far off and my head is buzzen from Monkey worken on it. It's peaceful and feels good to cry.

I don't know how long I'm there when Makepeace says Get up and he's standen over me, short and brown and built like a welterweight, got a big mustache and sideburns on him looks like a foreigner might have. There's white in the mustache and it shows up clear against the dark hair. One of the kids that saw the beaten must of went and got him out of the house and he come to get me. My mother was pregnant with Byron just then, the oldest of Makepeace's two boys.

Get up he says again. I'm still cryen and dribblen blood and I'm not about to give up on feelen sorry for myse'f just yet. I lay there and look at him for a time. He pokes at me with a boot that's crusted with manure and blood from Jeffries' slaughterhouse. Them boots is a crime to touch somebody with.

You leave me be I say.

He unstraps his belt off him and I can' believe he's about to whip me for getten beat by Monkey Granger. It's a great wide belt with his name, Curtis, tooled into the brown leather. The buckle is a bald eagle that clanks as he pulls the belt out from the loops.

You ain' gon' hit me I say but I'm none too sure.

You get up when I tell you he says. Or I will.

When I still lay there he brings the belt down and cracks me acrost the legs with it. I back away from him and stand.

You ain' got the right I say.

You gon' stop me he asks. He's swingen the belt from his hand and my legs sting like fire where he caught them. I don' want the belt again.

You got to learn he says. You got to learn sometime.

What's that I say. It's all I can get out I got my teeth clenched so tight against each other. I'm that mad that I can' hardly talk.

You got to keep on your feet he says. Most times it's all a man has that he can take what he takes standen up. Even if he can' give it back.

I'm gon' kill that damn Monkey Granger I say. I don' care what you say.

Makepeace shakes his head, standen there with the belt hangen down from his fist like a scourge. He looks like he's about to tell me somethen else but he don' say nothen to me.

*   *   *

Walken down Route 42 toward Gilchrist the air is cold enough to pain my lungs like knitten needles, the cold that you get just before dawn. With the hard freeze on us like this, I figure it will be too cold to snow and mebbe we will get a clear day out of it. It been overcast for a while and I will be glad to see the sun.

When I leave Doolittle's it is hard not to look back. I

keep thinken that Doolittle will be leanen out the door of the ratty old trailer or setten out at his metal shooten table, not wearen no shirt but bringen that thirty-ought-six to bear between my shoulder blades. It makes me itch back there but I don' scratch it.

Only when I get out of the holler and out onto the hardtop road again do I look back. The yellow dog that was in the yard is in the brush along the berm, moven along on its belly. It's got one eye that is clouded over like milk and they's a lot of gray in its muzzle whiskers.

Get home I say to it but it keeps followen me, tracken alongside me in the bushes, way down with its tail between its legs. It never does look away from me and that milky eyeball is beginnen to make me mad.

I go a little further with the dog comen after and then I lean down and grab some flat chunks of shale that are layen by the side of the road. I raise my hand to throw and the dog moves three-quarters away, looken over its shoulder. I figure from the way it acts that it seen some rocks thrown in its time. The dog stands there like that and still it don' go back.

I let fly and hit the leaves above the dog's head. The dog yarps like it been hit and skips off into the woods. I am glad to be rid of it but pocket a piece of the shale in case that it comes back.

I am just as glad not to of had to hit the thing. I wonder if it is Doolittle's dog or just hangen around there for the scraps it gets.

I would hitch a ride if I could but I am more then halfway into town when I see the first car on the road, headed in. It is a red low-rider and roars by in a hurry before I hardly get my thumb up. The breeze it makes passen presses my cold clothes against my skin. I hunch over and wish the sucker would blow out a tire and slide into the ditch but it don'. In just a minute it is around the curve at the end of the ridge and on into town.

When I get to town I am about wore out with walken. Still there ain' no lights on in any of the houses and stores and it seems to me like it ain' possible that all them people is still in bed. I go through town in the middle of the road, walken the double yellow line, and my feet hitten the blacktop is about all I can hear. The stoplight at the inter-section is set to blinken yellow my way, red the other. I wonder how long before it switches back to three colors for the day.

I am just about to the other side of town, tired enough that I nearly forget what I come to town for, when I see Makepeace's truck pulled to the curb at a slant. It is a four-by-four Dodge Ram with a heavy steel brush-guard on the front. Makepeace ain' inside.

The keys are in the ignition and it occurs to me to head back to the house. I got time to grab an hour or more sleep before I got to get to the slaughterhouse. We got all them hogs yet to do.

On the slick plastic seat it's a mess of blood I see. I get back out the truck and look around for Makepeace. He is in some trouble I now know. When I see him he is setten at the base of the Confederate soldier statue that the town built to honor the war dead from the county. He is got one arm acrost his belly and is grinnen at me. I go acrost to him. There is a lot of blood on his clothes and he closes his eyes.

You got trouble Curtis I say.

Oh mother he says and rocks back and forth. I got lost he says. This's all the farther I got.

He still got that arm acrost him and the blood runnen out from under it.

We gon' get you to County I say and bend to he'p him

up. He pulls at me to make me stop and there is more strength in the man then I would of thought. His blood has got on the concrete steps.

I known that fellow he says in my ear. His voice is strained, comes to me like he is far away. I tug at him again, get him up on his feet. The front of him is all blood and dirt; the round took him about the third shirt button. I check there ain' a hole in his back so the bullet is still in.

I drape his arm around my shoulders. He is a small man and I got to duck to help him. I got some muscle in my back from luggen beef and can carry him to the truck pretty much.

Eddy Sussen he says and he pulls us both around to half-face the statue. It is a twelve-foot-tall Reb soldier made out of bronze with the names of all the dead around the bottom. He's got him a club-shaped cap-and-ball rifle and it is pointen off at the horizon. Under the infantry cap you can see it is a good-looken face. The nose is long and straight and the features are even.

I shove Makepeace up into the cab of the truck and he grunts as I mash him past the oversize steeren wheel. In the passenger seat his head falls back and bangs against the rear glass hard enough to make me jump. I start the truck and pull it away from the square, head back up 42 toward the county hospital.

Gutshot Makepeace says looken down at what is comen from between his fingers. Like a goddam dog.

I keep my eyes on the road. The truck runs real good. Makepeace always has took fine care of it. I am all over his blood, down my jeans and I can feel some of it in one of my boots.

Et his gun Makepeace says.

What's that I say. He is mumblen and I can' believe he is still awake or still alive for that matter.

Eddy Sussen he says. Town council voted him in for the sculter to copy. He stood for that 'ere statue in '50 and then he et his gun in the square and it was a hell of a thing. I was fifteen and I seen what was left before they covered him up.

He was a good-looken boy I say. It is a thirty-mile drive to Heflin where the hospital is and it don' look any too good to me.

Makepeace snorts. Sure he was he says. Had him a crippled hand but that ain' in the statue.

Shoot I say.

Yeah he says. That mangled-up hand must of give him a lot of pain. He drunk a lot and one night he pulls the trigger on himse'f and he don' even get his name up on the statue.

Makepeace laughs and it is a terrible sound. That ain' the way to do it he says.

He is slumped in the corner of the truck cab and there is blood and snot bubblen out his nose. I can' even reach over and pick him up and set him straight if I want to keep the truck between the ditches.

Set up I say to him.

I can' he says to me. His eyes are closed and he don' even try to open them.

Set up I say again louder. He don' say nothen back to me and it don' look like any more bubbles comen out his nose that I can see. I shut my mouth and keep headen on down the road toward Heflin as fast as I can go even though there ain' any use in it.

Hackberry

Timmy Lee Purvis pulled off the road in front of the rented house, braked the old Buick to a stop. He stepped out the car, looked up at the porch, thinking to see Torrey coming down the steps toward him. She wasn't there. He tugged at the bill of his Goodrich cap with one big hand, pushed the car door closed. He leaned back against the side of the car. They'd had him doing a lot of toting down to the plant and it made him feel tired and old. He was just short of thirty, felt fifty or more.

"You ain' want to stay there like that," someone called from across the road. Timmy Lee turned, saw that it was the old guy who lived in the house on the other side of the narrow road. He was a small fellow wearing gray ratty coveralls, had skin that looked like jerked beef. Timmy Lee had seen him around the place, feeding the chickens he kept in a wire cage at the side of the house, cutting at some burdock near the road with a hoe. The old man was sitting on the front stoop of his place in an old cane-bottom chair tilted back against the wall. He had a glass of beer in one hand, resting it on his leg.

Timmy Lee pushed the sunglasses up on his nose,

looked at the old man. "What's that?" he called. His head hurt and he didn't want to talk. Their two houses—the one he had rented for him and Torrey and the old man's—were the only ones on that stretch of 42, about the only ones till you got into the subdivisions outside Gilchrist eight miles away. The old man spent a lot of his time on the front porch of his place, just sitting and looking.

"Just said you ain' want to leave your car there," the old man said. "On the shoulder like that. Get a lot of coal trucks highballen it thew here and the road's awful narrow." He settled back in his chair, took a sip of beer.

"Huh," Timmy Lee said. He'd heard the trucks himself in the evenings. You always heard the turbochargers first, that high whine way off like a gnat that is in your ear. Then the heavy Consolidated Mines ten-wheelers would roar through. He'd been surprised by the speed they could get up on the straight stretch, fully loaded like they were.

"Meant to tell you earlier but I never had the chance," the old man said. "Tole your wife." Timmy Lee got back in the car, backed it around so it stood square in the front yard, a good ten feet off the road. As he got out the Buick, he saw the dead yellow grass of the front yard. Have to remember to get some seed for that he thought. He'd meant to do it for a couple days, just couldn't seem to think of it when he was in town. He dug a toe into the dirt, saw how dry it was.

"That'll be good there. You're golden there," the old man said. Timmy Lee took off his sunglasses but the bright afternoon light hurt his head. He put them back on. "She ain' my wife," he said to the old man. The fellow's face tightened, creased up till it looked like a walnut or old apple. He didn't say anything back. "The girl you talked to, we ain' married or nothen," Timmy Lee said. He started up the porch steps.

"Well sure," the old man said to his back. "You bet.

Pretty little girl, her." Timmy Lee reached the porch door. The old man raised his glass of beer. "You mebbe want to crack a can?" he said. Timmy Lee thought it sounded like he was sorry for what he said. He shook his head.

"Don' think so, mister," he said.

"Hackberry," the old man said. "You call me Hackberry."

"I don' think today Hackberry," Timmy Lee said. He wondered if he had got the name right. It was an odd name. He opened the screen door, went on into the house.

"That's all right," the old man—Hackberry—yelled after him. "You come acrost some other day. Come when you get the time." The screen door slammed shut.

Timmy Lee sniffed the air of the house, couldn't smell anything cooking. He stepped into the front room, looked at the closed packing boxes spread around. Kitchen tools one had written on the side; clothes another one said; Xmas on the side of a third. Christmas lights and tinsel and an old pine wreath in that one, Timmy Lee knew. He nudged the box with his foot and something that was busted inside tinkled, a glass bulb most likely.

He took off his sunglasses, put them in the breast pocket of his work shirt. Tim the patch there said in red letters, above the Goodrich logo. Torrey was stretched out on the couch asleep. He smiled to see her, wearing jeans and a tee shirt, one of his. It was huge on her, near swallowed her up. She was just over five feet tall and tan and beautiful. She had high cheekbones and a pointed face. Timmy Lee thought how funny it was to hold her, like holding a kid against him.

He crouched next the sofa, sat back on his heels. "Torrey baby," he said, put a hand on her shoulder. "You got to get up." She stirred under his hand, sat up slowly. She pushed honey-colored hair out of her eyes, put delicate bare feet on the floor. Her toenails were painted shell pink.

"Jesus Christ, Timmy Lee," she said. She closed her eyes, licked her lips. "Why'd you wake me up for." Timmy Lee said nothing, sat next to her on the couch. She didn't face him. "I was haven the best dream," she said. She put her hands behind her neck, stretched till the joints popped.

"What kind of dream was that, baby?" Timmy Lee said. Torrey got up, stood at the window. "I was married to some real rich guy," she said. "He took care of me and all."

Timmy Lee looked down at the oak boards of the floor. They'd been hammered together with real wood pegs, looked like, instead of nails.

Torrey waited for him to say something. She sighed. "I knew you wouldn' get it, Timmy Lee," she said.

"Huh," Timmy Lee said. He rose, stepped over a couple packing cartons that were still closed with strapping tape, walked into the kitchen. "You got an idee about supper?" he said.

"I met that old guy acrost the way that sits on his porch all the time," Torrey said. She gestured out the window at the house across the road. Hackberry was still out there. "I went out front to the box to see did we have any mail and he yelled out to me." She smoothed the cotton tee shirt across her flat stomach. "I think he was flirten with me."

Timmy Lee opened the refrigerator, frowned when the light didn't go on. He tapped the plastic dome over the light with a finger. Torrey followed him into the kitchen. "You know what his name is?" she said. "You won' ever guess what his name is."

"Hackberry," Timmy Lee said. Torrey grimaced. "You ever hear the like," she said. "What kind of a name is Hackberry."

"We got some chicken," Timmy Lee said. He pulled a

cardboard bucket off the top shelf of the fridge, put it on the kitchen table. "And some milk." He put his nose to the top of the half-full carton, swished milk around inside. "Still smells ok," he said.

Torrey picked up a cold chicken wing from the bucket, put it back. "You not hungry?" Timmy Lee said. He rummaged around in the bucket, found a second joint, bit into it. Chewing, he held it out to Torrey. "Want some?" he said. She shook her head.

"I seen a bar in town looked like a nice place," Torrey said. Timmy Lee put the piece of chicken down on the table, drank from the carton. The milk hadn't gone over yet but it would soon. It left a greasy taste in his mouth.

"Thought I might ask about a job, see if they need somebody," Torrey said.

"Dancen," Timmy Lee said.

Torrey nodded. "Or bussen tables, pushen drinks." She moved her hips in a slow grind. "Bet I'm still good enough they'd hire me."

Timmy Lee threw the carton of milk at her and it caught her square in the chest, exploded like a bomb. Milk gushed down her front, splashed the kitchen table. A few drops spattered the stovetop, sprinkled Timmy Lee. Torrey staggered back, fetched up against the refrigerator. She blinked, wiped the half-rancid milk out of her face.

Just like it came, the rage left Timmy Lee and he almost had to laugh, looking at Torrey standing there in the puddle of milk blinking at him. There was even milk in her hair. She pressed a hand to her chest where the quart carton had hit her. She opened her mouth.

"Doll baby," Timmy Lee said and he took a step toward her. For a second she looked like she was going to hit at him. She brought her hands up like some little woman boxer.

"Get them hooks down," Timmy Lee said. He kept his

voice low and gentle. She dropped her arms and he grabbed her, held her to him. She stiffened against him and he tightened his grip on her. "You ain' want to do that kind of shit, baby," he said. "You don' need it." He felt his shirt grow damp with milk where he held her pressed against him.

* * *

"Where'd you ever get a name like Hackberry anyway," Timmy Lee said the first time he went over to Hackberry's to drink beer. The two of them were sitting out on the old man's porch, watching the heat lightning flash way up in the hills, miles off. There was no thunder.

Hackberry looked at Timmy Lee, smiled. He had one silver tooth up front that flashed when he opened his mouth. Timmy Lee wondered where he had got something like that put in. It looked grotesque, the bright metal in the dark of the old man's mouth. Hackberry hooted.

"Shoot boy," he said, "I don' know. Wherever it is my people come from when they come I guess. Or mebbe it was a name they took when they was in the hills. Only name I ever had though."

"You from up in the hills are you?" Timmy Lee said. The beer in his hand was sweating. He wiped his wet palm on his jeans.

"Yessir," Hackberry said. "From up the high hollers. I'm about the first one of 'em made it down to the valley." He looked at the porch and the house like it was something to be proud of, getting down to the valley. It made Timmy Lee want to laugh at him. "The rest of 'em, I figger they died out up there in the hills," Hackberry said.

"Shoot," Timmy Lee said. "Lost touch with 'em didn' you."

Hackberry nodded at him. "I had a teacher in school

one time," he said, "a real smart woman, her, that told me a Hackberry was a tree." He took a drink of his beer. The chickens on their roost next the porch chuckled in their sleep, heads tucked under their wings. The heat lightning turned the far hillsides blue.

"A little bitty fruit-bearen tree," Hackberry said. "Up to then I thought a Hackberry was just my daddy and my brothers and me. I didn' know that a Hackberry meant anything at all besides just that."

"I ain' got the least idee what a Purvis is," Timmy Lee said. Hackberry looked at him and brayed laughter till Timmy Lee thought the old man might give in and have a heart attack. It didn't seem like it was all that funny to him but watching Hackberry he started to laugh too. Pretty soon they were both laughing so loud that Torrey came out the rented house across the way and told them to shut the hell up.

*   *   *

Timmy Lee looked at Hackberry over on the other side of the porch. The old man fiddled one last time with the tuning knob on his radio, got the station that he wanted tuned in just right. It was a station out of the state capital, sounding tinny and weak with the distance. Some old black ladies were singing "Will the Circle Be Unbroken" and Timmy Lee figured they had just caught the tail end of a gospel program.

"This is right good," Hackberry said. "You gonna like this one." He sat back in his chair, picked his glass of beer up off the porch railing where he'd set it, took a long swallow.

It was the fifth or sixth night Timmy Lee had been across the road at Hackberry's since he'd met the old man the

week before. It had got to be a habit, coming over to sit
on the old man's porch, drinking beer and listening to the
radio, bullshitting. Hackberry seemed like he always knew
what program was going to be on.

Timmy Lee lit up one of the Tiparillos he liked. Hackberry's radio was an old tube job, must of weighed twenty
pounds or more. The metal grill over the speaker looked
like somebody had pulled it off the front end of an old
Plymouth.

"What is it we gon' listen to, Hackberry?" Timmy Lee
said. The tubes inside the radio glowed out through the
heat vents like angry orange eyes or tiny campfires. Timmy
Lee knew Hackberry had to be feeling some heat coming
off it but he didn't seem to mind.

"Answer man out of Charleston," Hackberry said. "You
should listen at this boy talk. Ain' nothen he can' tell a
person." The women stopped singing and the radio went
silent. For a minute Timmy Lee thought the old Philco had
gone dead or there was a problem at the station. Then the
sound came back, the answer man's music, and an announcer's voice said, "And here's Rich Hebron with Help
Talk. If you've got questions, legal, monetary, or just plain
personal, give Rich a call on our toll-free lines." The music
swelled up again after the announcer gave out the number
to call.

"What do you think about that?" Hackberry said.

"I ain' run acrost this one before," Timmy Lee said.

"It's a good un," Hackberry said. He put his hand on
top of the radio like he appreciated the warmth. Rich
Hebron came on, said he was ready to take the first caller.

"Reception's pret' good out of the capital," Timmy Lee
said. "For comen acrost the mountains."

Hackberry put a finger to his lips. "You want to listen
to this," he said.

"And our first call is from Hurricane," Rich Hebron said. He had a deep voice and he sounded tired. Timmy Lee could picture a cop having a voice like that or somebody's father. Rich pushed some buttons up in the capital, said "hello" twice. Finally a little old lady's voice came over the line.

"Rich?" she said. She sounded afraid, couldn't hear him for the first couple of seconds. Rich was patient with her, just said "hello" a couple of more times till she heard him.

"And what can we help you with tonight, ma'am?" the answer man said to the old lady when she got settled down. Hackberry leaned forward to hear her; her voice wasn't very loud above the crackle of the phone line. Timmy Lee wondered what problem an old woman like that could have.

"I got a grandaughter out here gone bad," the old woman said. Timmy Lee almost laughed. What was it she thought Rich Hebron was going to do about her grandaughter?

"That girl run aroun', I never see the like. Slut, she is getten to be. Easy, like."

Hackberry took a sip of beer and the Adam's apple worked in his skinny old throat.

"Her daddy gone off and her momma lef' her with me and I can' do nothen with her." Rich made a couple noises like he was going to interrupt but once the old woman had gotten started it didn't seem like she knew how to stop. "When them boys, them yahoos from the hollers come sniffen aroun' what's an old woman gon' do?" She was on the edge of tears. Hackberry moved in his hardback chair.

"Yes ma'am yes ma'am," Rich Hebron said but he sounded impatient. "But what specifically is the problem? I can understand why it is you're upset, sure I can, but I answer questions on this show. Do you have a question for me?"

"Question?" the old lady said. She stopped. Timmy Lee thought she was gone but he could still hear the hissing of the phone connection.

"Ma'am," Rich said. "You still there? You want to know what to do about the boys who are interested in your grandaughter, is that it? What advice you should give her?"

"What to do? Too late for advice, she gone and done it already. She gon' have a baby she keeps on like this, like her momma and with no daddy to bring it up. She was a good girl, she gone bad. What I'm s'posed to do with a girl like that?"

Rich sounded like he wanted to interrupt again but the woman kept on. "Ma'am," he said again but he couldn't stop her, and she was in tears now. Finally a commercial came up right in the middle of what she was saying. It was an ad for a Chevrolet dealership in the capital.

Hackberry kept looking at the radio, patting it with his hand. He wouldn't look at Timmy Lee.

"You say that there's a good radio answer man?" Timmy Lee said. He dented the sides of his aluminum beer can with his strong fingers, laughed. "Didn' have too many answers for that old lady."

"Mebbe she'll be back on," Hackberry said. "It's just a commercial." The Chevy ad ended and Rich Hebron came back on the radio. This time he was talking to a guy from St. Albans. The guy had a neighbor that had said he'd take a shot at the man's dog if it got on his property. The guy on the radio asked Rich if that was legal.

"Got rid of her," Timmy Lee said. "Guess that's one kind of answer ain' it?"

Rich said, "Well sir, I can only tell you that it's legal to dispose of encroaching animals when the animals pose a threat to life, livestock or property."

"You mean he can kill my dog if he wants?" the guy from St. Albans wanted to know.

"It is however illegal to discharge firearms within city limits. If your neighbor does that," Rich said, "you should call the police. Meantime you should probably keep your dog on a leash."

Rich clicked the guy off the line before he could say anything. Timmy Lee figured the incident with the old woman had unsettled him some. He didn't want any back talk.

"That old woman should of knew better then to act like that on the radio," Hackberry said. "You can' expect Rich to answer questions like that. Ask him about a lawn-mower engine or what to take for a fever or," he gestured at the radio, "your dog and he can tell you. Not about stuff like that old lady wanted."

"Huh," Timmy Lee said. "What good's it gon' do that guy to call the police after the neighbor shoots his dog, Hackberry? Strikes me this Rich guy ain' much in the way of an answer man."

"Yeah well," Hackberry said. He snapped the radio off in the middle of another of Rich's answers: he was talking to a fat man that wanted to lose weight to get women. He figured they didn't like the way he looked. After a couple of seconds the hot orange light of the tubes began to die out.

"It ain' Rich," Hackberry said. "It's them people. Them folks that call in, they just ain' asken the right questions."

*   *   *

As Timmy Lee walked up to his front porch he saw a garbage bag lying in the yard. He'd left not long after Hackberry switched off Rich Hebron's radio show. The old man had pretty much shut up after that. Timmy Lee hadn't meant to piss him off: he just hadn't thought it was much of a show, that was all.

He bent and picked the garbage bag up. Most of the trash had fallen out of it, but there was some left: a couple frozen orange juice containers, beer cans, egg shells. The bag was wet where Timmy Lee held it. He balled it up, walked around the house to where the two metal garbage cans were.

One of the cans was on its side, the lid a few feet away. "Dogs," he said, picked the can up, pitched the wet bag inside. "Had to of been dogs." He grinned, thinking about that guy from St. Albans that had called the answer man. Timmy Lee didn't blame the neighbor so much.

He wiped his hand on his jeans. There was garbage all over the place, paper sacks and old magazines, leftover food. He picked some of it up, tossed it in the can too. He left a lot of it lying on the ground, figured he'd get it in daylight, tell Torrey to pick it up. He wanted to wash his hands, get the sticky juice off. He went into the house through the back door into the kitchen.

Torrey was in there, standing in front of the sink. She turned as he came in. "Oh," she said. Timmy Lee nodded to the door. "Dogs must of got in the garbage," he said. "Scattered it to hell, all over the yard." He went to the sink but Torrey stood half in his way. When he looked at her she moved.

The sink was full of ashes, looked like, sticky black ashes and water. "What the hell's this?" Timmy Lee said. Torrey took another step back, rubbing at her eyes. They were red with crying. "I done some baken," she said.

The drain was stopped up; she'd been trying to wash the stuff down the sink. Timmy Lee could smell something burned. The stink was bad but must of been worse not long before. Timmy Lee forgot about washing his hands. "What'd you try to put it down the sink for?" he said.

"I made spoon bread but it burned," Torrey said. "You know how you like it. It was in the oven and them dogs come around the back and all. They was in the yard and I could hear 'em howlen and barken, tearen things up. I went out and it was a bunch of mutts, five or more, and one little yellow bitch that must of been in heat. They was all over her like ants, you know how they do, so I took out after 'em with a stick." She paused. "I knew you was gon' be mad."

"Why didn' you thow it out the back door with the rest of the trash?" he said. "Just pitch it out in the yard."

"I knew you'd be pissed," she said, "and I just thew it in the sink. I tried to get rid of it." She was crying. Timmy Lee couldn't stand it.

He stepped forward, grabbed a handful of her hair, pulled her head back. She blinked, tried not to look at him. He shook her. "Why'd you do this?" he said. She twisted her head, tried to get loose.

"You let me go," she said, pushing at his wrist. He shook her hard one last time, shoved her away. He turned back to the mess in the sink. It was going to be hell to clean up and she wasn't going to do it, that was a bet. He put a finger in the burned spoon bread. It was still warm. Torrey walked out of the kitchen.

Timmy Lee turned on the faucet, ran a little water into the sink to see if maybe it would clear the drain. He put his hands under the flow of water, rubbed them together. The water in the sink rose.

"I had enough," Torrey shouted from the bedroom. "You ain' doen this to me no more." Timmy Lee put his wet hands against his cheeks. The water was cool, felt good. He flicked water from his hands back into the sink, tried not to look at the spoon bread. It was black and softening in the water.

"I ain' gon' set aroun' all the time, let you beat on me," Torrey said. "Get drunk with some old man and never see me then come home and beat on me." Timmy Lee left the kitchen, went to the bedroom. Torrey was going in the closet, pulling her stuff out, tossing it on the bed. He tried to smile.

"Where you goen?" he said. She didn't answer him, tossed a skirt down on the bed. Timmy Lee picked it up, smoothed it over his arm. "I think you're goen nowhere," Timmy Lee said.

"You stoppen me?" Torrey said. She kept the bed between her and Timmy Lee. She quit fiddling with her clothes, looked up at him, arms crossed. Timmy Lee nodded. "I stopped you before," he said. "Stopped you a bunch of times before."

"I was a kid then," Torrey said.

"What is it you want me to do?" Timmy Lee said.

"I don' care," Torrey said. "I ain' want nothen from you. Not anymore. I try to do you somethen nice and you beat on me."

Timmy Lee came around the bed. Torrey backed away from him. He pressed himself against her, pushed her to the wall. "You ain' want to go nowhere," he said. He put his lips on hers. She turned her head away.

"I'm goen," she said. Timmy Lee picked her up off the floor a little way, kissed her again. This time she didn't turn away so fast. "I'm goen," she said into his mouth. "I got places to go. You ain' stoppen me."

*   *   *

"I keep haven this dream, Hackberry," Timmy Lee said. It had been a few day since Torrey tried to make the spoon bread and she wasn't talking about leaving anymore.

Timmy Lee felt like he couldn't stand it when she talked about leaving.

He'd had a few beers and he felt fine, his head felt clear. He squinted at the old man on the other side of the porch, couldn't tell if he was listening or not. Hackberry hadn't brought the radio out onto the porch in a while.

"Nightmare more like," Timmy Lee said. "It ain' a good dream." He couldn't believe how sober he felt after the beer he'd drunk.

"It's about Torrey," he said. He looked at his watch but it was too dark to see the hands. He thought about the dream, tried to remember it. He'd had it a bunch of times but it was hard to remember dreams sometimes. He'd told it to Torrey once and she'd laughed.

"I'm standen in this field of clover, smells just great," he said. "That's one thing I do know is the good smell. And not too far off there's this old locust fence post—you can tell it's locust—tilted over in its hole loose as a rotted tooth." Timmy Lee could see that Torrey had shut off all the lights at his rented house.

He brought the can of beer up to drink but it was empty. He crushed the can flat, sidearmed it at the house across the way. It fell short, hit the road instead. It took a bounce on the blacktop, rolled a little way, stopped. Timmy Lee reached down, grabbed a full can off the pack.

"There's a big crow, giant crow, big as a wild turkey setten on the locust post, and it's Torrey. She's setten on this old loose fence post and she's looken at me with this crow's little shiny black eye." Timmy Lee got up from his chair, looked in one of Hackberry's porch windows. The house was dark and he could only see a reflection of himself in the glass: no eyes or nose or mouth but just the shape of his face on the window. He didn't know what the inside of Hackberry's house looked like.

"Way down in the field seems like there's always a flock of other crows, setten in the trees of the windbreak, and they're maken one hell of a racket. This big crow's just looken at me so I run at it and yell, just shout at it. I'm goen to try to put my hands on it and it all the time looks like I'm goen to get it too."

Timmy Lee thought about the crow, its dark eye, the tongue like a big gray nightcrawler in the half-open beak, the scaled claws holding onto the hard wood of the fence post.

"But then that fricken crow takes off, just strokes up into the air and it's gone," he said. Hackberry shifted his weight in the chair and Timmy Lee waited for him to say something. He didn't.

"All the rest of them do the same, like there's a signal." He paused, recalled something else about the dream. "Weird thing," he said. "When that big crow takes off I'm just close enough to smell it over the smell of the clover, to smell what comes off its wings. Know what it is?"

"Dust," he said. "Comen out the feathers, dry old yard dirt. Ain' that the damnedest? A dusty crow." He laughed. "Hey Hackberry, what the hell. That crow," he said.

"You know what I used to listen to on the radio all the time?" Hackberry said. His eyes were closed. He leaned back in his chair. "Greatest damn show was ever on the radio."

Timmy Lee didn't think Hackberry had been listening when he was talking before. He didn't mind.

"'Mr. Keane, Tracer of Lost Persons,'" Hackberry said. "That guy was great, that Mr. Keane. He could find anybody or anything, boy. He had him some tough cases and he solved ever one of 'em. Don' you tell me."

"Better then some radio answer man, huh?" Timmy Lee said.

Hackberry opened his eyes. "Yeah boy, better then any answer man. Mr. Keane could tell 'em where things was at. You ever hear that show, Timmy Lee?"

"Naw," Timmy Lee said.

"I didn' figure you would of," Hackberry said. "That was a long time ago. Same radio though," he said. "Same radio."

"Still," Timmy Lee said, "what good does that Mr. Keane do you? I mean, that's just a show. Some guy wrote that to come out the way it did." He saw that Hackberry wasn't looking at him.

"Hell, I know that," Hackberry said.

The two men were silent for a while. Finally Hackberry looked up. He kept his eyes on Timmy Lee, made him a little nervous. "Hold your hands up," Hackberry said to Timmy Lee.

"What?" Timmy Lee said.

"Hold your hands up there for me to look at a second," Hackberry said. Timmy Lee held his hands up, palms out. Hackberry twirled a finger. "Other way," he said.

Timmy Lee turned the backs of his hands to Hackberry. "What you doen, Hackberry?" he said.

The old man pursed his lips. "You a fighter ain' you, Timmy Lee," he said.

"I been in some scrapes," Timmy Lee said.

"You pretty good though, huh," Hackberry said.

"I figger I can take care of myself. What the hell are you talken about?" He lowered his hands, folded them one against the other in his lap. Hackberry leaned forward.

"I known that about you," Hackberry said. "Known it about you the first time ever I seen you, that you could take care of yourself. That's good."

"Huh," Timmy Lee said.

"Naw, I'm serious," Hackberry said. "That's one thing

I wasn' ever any good at was fighten. Got out of some mix-ups the hard way," he said. He clapped his hands together.

"Took it on the head sometime huh?" Timmy Lee said. He couldn't picture skinny old Hackberry swinging on anybody.

"Yeah," Hackberry said. "One time some guy knocked me down and then he put a blade into me. Can you believe that? He already beat me and he cuts me into the bargain. Big old pigsticker too, with the blade that come straight out the handle when he pushed a button. Must of been six, eight inches long."

"Son bitch," Timmy Lee said. "Where'd he put it in?"

"Stuck me right here." Hackberry raised his right arm, put his left hand up under the armpit. "There's still a hell of a scar. Here, you want to feel it?"

"Naw," Timmy Lee said. "I believe you, Hackberry. Damn. Why would a man do that?"

"He was drunk. So was I, what the hell. But he put it to me, right into the lung, 'cause I couldn' stop him from doen it to me. That's when they'll get you, the only time, is when you can' stop 'em from doen it. You got to watch out."

"Yeah," Timmy Lee said. He thought about that, being down and having some bastard put the knife to you.

"You ain' got to worry about that, though," Hackberry said. "Not a big boy like you."

"No," Timmy Lee said. They'd never get the chance, he knew. He'd do it to them first.

"Know what it's like when you get the blade put to you?" Hackberry said. He was leaning forward, looked like he was grinning. The silver tooth shone in the dark. He kept his hand up under his arm where the scar was.

"You can taste it," Hackberry said. "When it hits the lung like that, you can just taste it." He wiped his mouth with his hand. "Tastes like metal," he said. "Tastes like a goddam pewter cup."

* * *

When he was twenty-five Timmy Lee met Torrey at a bar in the Ohio Valley. He was out there on his vacation visiting with some of his buddies from the Army. He'd spent most of his enlisted time stationed in Korea and all he knew about the Army was it was cold out there and very boring peacetime duty. His buddies had been there with him and all of them knew they never did want to go back. They all agreed strongly on that one point.

Torrey was dancing up on the narrow stage that the bar had. It was called the Emerald Room and everything in it was green—green velvet, green wallpaper, green plastic plants—or shaded green by the green lights they had on sconces all around the room. She was dancing with two other girls up there and all of them swinging their haunches to some cheesy music that was on the stereo, looking bored and stoned out of their minds.

Timmy Lee and his buddies yelled and called at them and never really did notice what they looked like, just that they were women that were mostly naked standing on the stage up there nearby, sweating under the lights. They knew that the two bouncers by the door had sacks of ball bearings in their pockets and would sap them if they tried to climb up on the stage with the dancers or touch them in any way. That made them yell, shout at the women whatever came into their heads.

Then things got real busy, a softball game let out and the whole winning team came in and their families and all their friends, seemed like, and the place got wild. The

manager got the two other girls that were on the stage
with Torrey to come down and throw on aprons and run
around waiting tables. They smelled hot, like burned hair,
when they got near Timmy Lee. He figured it was from
the lights. One of them was old viewed close up, in her
forties maybe, and it embarrassed him to see a woman of
her age doing that kind of thing, he wasn't quite sure why.

Torrey was up there by herself and for a minute after
the other two women left she stopped dancing and just
stood and looked at the crowd. She was tiny standing
under the lights, the dust and the smoke thick around her
so you could hardly see, it was like she was standing in a
cloud. She had her hip cocked and one hand braced against
it. Her mouth was open and her teeth were small and
perfect. Then she bit at her lip, sucked it into her mouth,
and started to dance on the stage, all alone.

Timmy Lee watched her while his buddies roared and
tried to grab the other two dancers and whatever women
came close to them. The softball players got drunk quickly
and started causing some trouble and there might of been
a fight over one of the guys pinching somebody else's wife
if the big bouncers hadn't been there. Timmy Lee missed
it all, watching Torrey.

The dance was clumsy and stupid, like a girl dancing
by herself at a junior-high prom, twirling, toes pointed,
step in, step out. She almost fell once and she looked up
with her face red. Nobody noticed and that made Timmy
Lee feel even worse for her. "I'm watchen you," he wanted
to shout out. "You dance and I'll watch and we can let all
of these others just go down to hell alone." He didn't say
anything though and a couple minutes later the manager
came up and told Torrey to get down, go around and wait
on the tables. Nobody yelled when she got down off the

stage, nobody at all told her to get back up there and finish her dance.

*   *   *

Timmy Lee started, sat up in the chair. The night air was cool but the back of his neck, the collar of his shirt were damp with sweat. "Jesus," he said. He shook his head, leaned forward in the chair. His stomach hurt. He figured it was from not eating, from drinking on an empty belly. "Hackberry?" he said. He turned to the old man.

Hackberry's glass of beer lay on its side on the porch floor. It had been empty when it tipped over; wasn't any puddle. Hackberry was dead asleep in his chair, snoring. Too much beer Timmy Lee thought. He considered waking Hackberry up, decided to let it go. He looked at Hackberry's neck, the loose webbed skin, the bags under his eyes. Hackberry was sitting back in his chair; his left hand was caught under his right arm, up near the armpit. Timmy Lee shook his head.

He wondered if Hackberry spent many nights asleep on the porch. It made him a little sad. He sat his beer can down, ran a hand through his hair. He didn't feel tired at all anymore. He felt good, like he had an edge to him. "Little drink might help that edge, wouldn't hurt at all," he said to himself. Away at the end of the straight stretch he heard a coal truck change up into a high gear. "Drivers are still out," he said. "Not everbody's in bed."

He stepped off the porch, walked down to the edge of the road. The beer can that he had thrown was still there, just on the opposite side of the blacktop. Timmy Lee waited for the truck to pass.

It roared up on him, lights flicking to bright and then down again. Timmy Lee thought the truck swerved closer to his side of the road as it went by. He wasn't scared. The truck's wake smelled of diesel fuel and chips of coal from the over-full bed pattered off his shoulders.

He crossed the road, looking for the crushed beer can. He wanted to kick it, wanted to hear the empty metal sound it would make as it bounced down the road. The truck had swept it off the blacktop so he looked for it in the high grass of the berm. After a while of not finding it he quit looking.

* * *

"It ain' just the tires for the airplanes, hell no it ain'," Timmy Lee told her, standing next the bar in the Emerald Room. He'd found out her name was Torrey Pinch and told her that he never heard the name Torrey before. She claimed nineteen and to be in the community college but he knew she wasn't old enough to have graduated high school. He didn't say that he thought she was lying though and she seemed to appreciate that. He didn't ask her what somebody that young was doing dancing in a red-neck bar either.

"We make the whole entire wheel assembly at Goodrich," he said. "Hydraulic struts and wheels and brakes as well as tires. It's a vital part of the defense industry." That was what they told them at the plant pep talks, when the plant manager tried to get morale and productivity up. Torrey was leaning against the bar with a tray of empties in her one hand and looking at him like she gave a damn. He was happy to see that.

"F-14s, F-15s, B-52s, wouldn' none of 'em get in the air or back down again if it wasn' for us," he said. "It's like I'm up there with 'em, in a way, ever time I torque a bolt onto the assembly, if you can see it that way."

"You bet," she said. She looked over his shoulder to make sure Ernie, the guy who ran the bar, wasn't watching her stand there and jaw while softball players wanted drinks.

"Sometime," Timmy Lee said, "sometime I think about them wheels and where they'll go. Think about the boys that are up there in them fast airplanes and how they need them wheels to give them a way back to the earth. Or the carrier or whatever."

"Like you was a flyer or somethen," she said. "That's real exciten and romantic." He looked at her and couldn't believe that somebody as pretty as her thought he was exciting. He hadn't ever seen an F-15 except on tv or in the movies. "Ain' nothen that ever goes on aroun' here," she said to him, and her voice was flat and uninflected. He wondered if dancing left her tired. "Just softball games is all that they like to do around here. You about the best thing to come in here in a long time."

He went back to the Emerald Room the next night to see her, and there wasn't a softball team to come in and make noise and trouble. He left his Army buddies behind, didn't tell them where he was going at all. After she finished dancing, she came down to his table and sat with him and joked till Ernie ran her off into the back to tend the grill.

The next night he came back to see her again and the night after that he had to leave back for Gilchrist, had to get back to work. She came down to the bus station to see him off and that was a nice surprise for him and a little sad too. He hadn't expected that at all. She was wearing a yellow wraparound skirt and a white blouse and he told her he thought she was beautiful. When the bus pulled out, she was sitting in the seat next to him, her arm on his, talking and giggling and pleased as hell to get out of the Ohio Valley.

* * *

The only place in Gilchrist that looked like being open when Timmy Lee drove into town was called The Pioneer. Timmy Lee hadn't ever been in it before. He always went to a place called The Black Bear, right across from Goodrich. He didn't want to see The Black Bear, didn't want to see Goodrich, not then. He figured he'd see it early enough in the morning. A sign on the front of The Pioneer said "Girls Girls Girls."

He walked into the bar. When the door whacked closed behind him, a couple of guys sitting at a table in the corner turned, looked him over. They were the only people in the place. One of them was tall, wearing a fringed shirt, tan like buckskin with rawhide laces on the front.

The other was wearing an old Airmobile jacket even though it was warm in the bar. All the insignia had been cut off the jacket and there were light-colored places on the sleeves where the stripes had been. Looked like master sergeant but the guy that was wearing the jacket wasn't old enough. He looked straight at Timmy Lee, tried to stare him down. After a few seconds he looked away, spoke to the guy at the table with him.

There was a small platform, looked like a stage, on one side of the room. It was a box, about ten feet on a side with a couple of steps up to it. There was some indoor-outdoor carpet laid down on the stage floor.

Timmy Lee looked around for a waitress, couldn't see one. There was just a fat guy in a stained white apron behind the bar. He had a sleepy eye and a round pale face, pocked like the moon. He moved real slow.

Timmy Lee climbed onto one of the bar stools. "Grill's closed. Bar's closen in a couple minutes," the fat guy said. He was chewing a mint toothpick. He picked up a rag off the bar, wiped a highball glass with it. The glass squeaked when the guy rubbed it and the noise bothered Timmy Lee. He looked at the bartender to see if he was making the noise just to be irritating.

"You got time to give me a drink," Timmy Lee said. The fat guy didn't move. He had a fringe of beard on his face, no mustache. It made his face look dirty. He set the highball glass down.

"Shot of Black Jack and a beer," Timmy Lee said. Behind him he could hear the two guys at the table. It sounded like they were arguing. They kept their voices low. The bartender looked over at them, shook his head.

"You gon' give me that shot?" Timmy Lee said. The fat guy filled a glass with beer, set it down in front of Timmy Lee. It took him a while to find the bottle of Black Jack under the bar. He poured a shot, put the small glass next the beer. "Buck seventy," he said.

Timmy Lee picked the shot glass up, held it in two fingers over the beer, dropped it in. The small glass sank to the bottom of his mug. A little beer splashed the bar and Timmy Lee thought the bartender shot him a look out of his good eye. The bad eye wandered all around the walls of the place. Timmy Lee drank about half the glass, wiped his mouth with the back of his hand. "Jesus," he said. He felt his head start to ache again; he was tired, wished he hadn't come into town after all. He hoped his head would clear.

"Buck seventy," the bartender said again.

Timmy Lee pulled his wallet out of his back pocket. He had to get off the stool to do it. He felt unsteady, braced against the bar. He paid the bartender. "You feelen ok?" the fat guy asked. He didn't really care. He shifted the toothpick from one side of his mouth to the other.

Timmy Lee sat back down on the stool, planted his hands on the bar on either side of his drink. The Black Jack eddied in the glass like dirty water, a color darker than the beer. Timmy Lee nodded toward the stage. "You got girls? Like it says outside?"

The fat guy took the toothpick out his mouth, dropped it in an ashtray on the bar. It looked soft and chewed. "What, dancers?" he said to Timmy Lee.

"Yeah," Timmy Lee said. "Dancers, you know, strippers."

"Thursday, Friday, Sat'day night we got dancers," the bartender said. He looked at the toothpick in the ashtray like he was sorry he got rid of it. "This's Tuesday so no dancers." He considered. "They only get down to these g-string bikinis is all the law allows," he said, "so I don't know if you'd rightly call them strippers. Now I used to work at a place down to Charlotte that they got them stripped all the way down."

"Huh," Timmy Lee said. He wondered whether the guy would give him another drink or not. He looked at the stage, at the mini-spots hanging from the rafter above it. They were different colors—red, yellow, blue—but they were turned off. "Goddam," he said.

"You like that, do you, them dancers?" the fat guy asked. He leaned closer than Timmy Lee liked, breathed in his face. His breath smelled like spring ramps. The pores of his face were huge. Timmy Lee turned away, looked out over the room.

The guy in the Airmobile jacket brought his fist down on the table where he was sitting. It made the glass in front of him jump, tip over. Ice spilled across the table top. He leaped up from his chair to keep from getting a lapful of ice and the guy in the fringed shirt laughed. "God," he said, "you are a dumb-ass." His voice was loud. The guy in the military jacket narrowed his eyes.

"Them girls now," the bartender said from behind Timmy Lee. It startled him, the voice so close behind his ear. "A man might could get to know a girl or two if he had a mind." Timmy Lee didn't want to turn, to see the fat sweaty face with the crazy eye so close in back of him. He watched the other men in the bar instead.

The fellow in the military jacket brushed ice and water off his chair onto the floor, sat again. He looked angry. The other guy was relaxed. He was still laughing a little.

The bartender put a hand on Timmy Lee's shoulder. "You want I should make a phone call?" he said. "Tuesday night, somebody's gon' be free to give you a date. Won' be cheap but somebody's gon' be available."

Timmy Lee moved his shoulder but the fat guy kept his hand there. The hand was soft and Timmy Lee could feel the fat fingers pressing into the flesh of his shoulder. It was like a possum climbing on him. "You want to move that hand," Timmy Lee said, not very loud.

The fat guy didn't seem to hear. "Just for you, special-like," he said.

"You want to move that hand," Timmy Lee said again. He half-stood and the fat guy put pressure behind the flabby hand, tried to force Timmy Lee back down onto the stool. "Whoa up now," he said.

Timmy Lee shook the hand off, faced the bartender. "Keep your damn hands off me," he said. The fat guy held his hands up, showing Timmy Lee they weren't anywhere near him. Timmy Lee took a sip of his drink, put the glass down. He was ready to leave.

Before he could go the guy in the military jacket moved in front of him. Timmy Lee hadn't even heard him get up from his chair. "What's the problem here, hoss?" he said. He tapped Timmy Lee on the chest, pushed him a little. The guy in the fringed shirt was watching. The guy in the Airmob jacket looked over his shoulder at him, then back at Timmy Lee. He was smiling.

Timmy Lee hit him in the face. It was a sloppy right cross but the other guy wasn't ready for it. Timmy Lee felt the nose pop, felt the lips split. Something let go in his hand and the pain, so clear all the way up to his elbow, was like a revelation. He shook his hand and the pain stayed with him. It cleared his head.

"Shit," the guy said and he put his hands to his face. The word sounded funny through his busted mouth.

Then the tall guy in the fringed shirt was all over Timmy Lee, elbows and knuckles. Timmy Lee swung at him but the swing went wild.

The tall man stepped back, took his time, kicked Timmy Lee square in the stomach. The kick was graceful, like a dancer's move, karate maybe. Timmy Lee fell back into the bar, knocked over a couple bar stools. He could hear the bartender cursing.

The tall guy kicked him again and Timmy Lee felt his arm go numb. The guy kept kicking. It seemed like he kicked Timmy Lee forever. All the time he was kicking Timmy Lee could hear the bartender yelling at him to stop and the guy with the busted face saying "Shit" over and over through his split lips.

* * *

Timmy Lee pulled the car off the road at an angle, didn't give a damn about the coal trucks. He looked up at Hackberry's porch, saw that the old man had gone inside. He wished Hackberry was still out on the porch to help him. He opened the car door, looked at his watch in the light from the overhead dome. He blinked, feeling stupid, realized that the face of the watch had gotten smashed in the fight. The hour hand was gone.

He got out of the car, leaned against it. He put his head down on the metal of the roof. It was cool, felt good against his battered face. His legs were rubbery and weak. It made him sick, the way his knees wobbled. He burped, spit a little blood and mucus onto the car. He felt in his mouth where a couple of teeth were gone. He was afraid to touch the spot with his tongue. The taste in his mouth was awful.

He turned from the car, made it across the yard to the steps of the house. He climbed the first step, then sat. The feeling was coming back into the right side of his face. It had felt strange all the way home, like it wasn't part of his head at all. He put his hand up to his face and it felt lumpy. He closed his eyes against the sick feeling in his belly.

He stood again, holding on to the porch railing, tried to open the screen door. He couldn't. He tugged on it, knew that Torrey had latched the door from the inside. He rattled the door in its frame, almost fell. "Torrey," he said. He tried to yell. "Let me the hell in." It was almost a whisper. He knew no one would hear him.

He bunched his hand into a fist, pounded on the door. The hand was clumsy, flopped on his wrist. He couldn't feel it. Two of his knuckles were sunk into the flesh, misshapen. Blood oozed from where the watch crystal had cut him. He knew he had broken the knuckles when he hit the guy in the military jacket. He had broken knuckles before. They never seemed to heal just right.

He put his face up to the window, looked into the living room of the rented house. Torrey looked out at him. She said "Oh"—he could hear it through the glass—and skipped back away. She almost fell over one of the packing cartons.

"Torrey," he said. He leaned his forehead against the window. The glass was cool, like the roof of the car. He said her name again. A little blood flecked the window glass when he spoke.

Torrey stood just inside the door to the front room, staring at him. He gestured at the porch door and she shook her head. He brought his hand up, tried to put it through the window, but it wouldn't curl into a fist anymore.

"You bastard," Torrey said from inside. "What you done?" The words came to him like she had said them underwater. He didn't understand them. Torrey ran from the living room, disappeared into the back of the house.

Timmy Lee thought about sitting on the porch in the cool night air. He knew that if he sat he wouldn't get up again but he wasn't sure he cared. He stumbled, fell down the porch stairs, fell in his front yard. The dirt there was dry and loose and it covered his clothes, caked in the blood on his face, his hands. He got back in the car, sat in the driver's seat. The vinyl creaked under his weight.

He looked around the inside of the car, moved the rear-view mirror so he could see his face. He was a mess. One of his ears was near torn off. That was why the side of his head felt so bad. Blood from the ear was everywhere: his neck, down his collar, in his hair, his eyebrows even. He almost laughed, he looked so terrible.

He put his hand on the knobs of the radio, wondered what Rich Hebron would tell him to do. Sue the suckers he figured. Call the police. Unless it was legal; maybe he'd been endangering life or property. What the hell.

Hackberry's house was just too far away. He knew he

could never make the distance. His legs wouldn't carry him that far. He pictured himself passed out in the middle of the blacktop and a highballing coal truck coming along the straight stretch. No sir. Ah God why hadn't she let him in?

He put the heel of his hand against the horn ring, pressed. The sound was loud in the dark and he took his hand away. His heart was pounding. He put his hand back, pressed the horn again. Hackberry would hear.

A light in Hackberry's house clicked on and Timmy Lee smiled. The chickens in the pen next the house clucked and stirred at the noise. After a second the light went out again. Timmy Lee stopped smiling, kept his broken hand pressed hard against the horn of the old Buick.

Dog

E ldridge heard the noise before Broom did. Broom was watching cartoons on the little black-and-white tv on the floor in the living room and he had the sound up pretty high so he missed it.

The noise that Eldridge heard was a squeak, a high squeak and a scratching sound. He was coming out of the bathroom when he heard it, walking in his bare feet, just a towel wrapped around his waist. He figured at first it was the floor of the trailer—it was an old trailer that he and Broom lived in and beginning to rust out a little, starting to settle down uneven on the cinder-block foundations. Then he heard it again when he was a little ways down the hall toward the biggest bedroom and he knew this time that it was something that was alive.

"Yo Broom," he yelled down the hall into the living room. He could hear the tv in there, knew Broom probably wouldn't call back to him even if he heard. He and Broom had lived together in the trailer a couple years. He had got to know Broom pretty well. "Broom," he called again.

"We got rats, Broom." He walked on down the hall into his bedroom.

Broom came in after him a second later. He had a can of beer in his hand. Starting earlier and earlier in the day Eldridge thought. It was a bad habit to get into. Eldridge never touched the stuff before lunch, couldn't even hardly stomach a Coca-Cola before lunch. "What's that," Broom said. The tv roared away in the living room.

"I say we got rats," Eldridge said. "Or somethen." He stomped on the floor hard, trying to get the rats or whatever to make the noise again. The one window in the bedroom rattled in its frame. "Jesus," Broom said. "You like to knock the whole place down." He was a skinny kid was Broom, twenty-one or two, Eldridge wasn't sure which. He looked young though, always got carded in bars. It was pretty funny to watch his face when a bartender would say, "I gotta see some ID." It really pissed Broom off and his face would work and crease while he dug in the pocket of his jeans for his wallet. He was still having a bad time with acne and his face was ugly to see when he got mad, all red and mottled and looking like a goddam map of Mars.

He stood still for a second, tilted his head toward the floor like a rabbit dog. Eldridge was quiet, listening too. The only sound was music from the tv. "I don' hear nothen," Broom said. "No rats."

"Jest listen a while," Eldridge said. He pulled on a tee shirt. He wore a lot of tee shirts, muscle-shirts he called them, about a size too small with the sleeves cut off at the shoulder. Some girl one time or another had told him she liked that "sculpted" look. He had never forgot that, would say it from time to time to Broom or whoever, "I got that sculpted look." Pretty much whoever he said it to thought he was a jerk about his looks. He was average, except for the muscles, the washboard stomach and the thick arms. He never told anybody about the girl who had told him she thought he looked "grotesque." Never said a word about that.

"I heard it," Eldridge said. "Scratchen against the floor."

"Huh," Broom said. He started to head back to his tv show. Then the sound came again, seemed like it came from right under Eldridge's room this time. Broom heard it: a scratch and a whine. "There you go," Eldridge said. "There it is." He was pleased that Broom had heard it.

"Ain' rats," Broom said.

"What do you mean," Eldridge said. "If it ain' rats what is it?"

"I don' know but it ain' rats," Broom said. He paused a second like he was thinking. "Sound to me like a dog. Sound to me like we got a dog under the trailer."

"How you think it got there?" Eldridge said. Now that he thought about it the noise had seemed a lot like a dog to him too.

"Crawled under I guess. Maybe looken for some place jest to lay down and die. Maybe it's sick, maybe shot, I ain' got the least idee."

"I guess we got to go see then don' we?" Eldridge said. He leaned into his closet, shoved some clothes that were on the floor in there to one side, moved a couple boxes. He looked up on the shelf in the closet too. "Where's that flashlight," he said, "the big hunten lamp. What'd you do with the damn flashlight."

"Hell if I know," Broom said. "Last time I had it was last fall, last November. We were out spotlighten some deer, you 'member, with Fat Ed and that whole gang. Got us a couple too didn' we? Yeah, we sure ate all right after that for a while. Old Fat Ed's deer meat chili. Goddam."

"Yeah," Eldridge said. He had gone under the bed now

looking for the light. "But then what'd we do with it? Jesus," he said. He came back out from under the bed holding the lamp. It was a big Black and Decker that you could either run off its six-volt battery or plug into your cigarette lighter like a police light. It had deer blood on the handle and on the green plastic shock-proof case. Eldridge flicked at the blood with his fingertips and some of it flaked off onto the floor.

"That was under your bed?" Broom said. "It must of smelled like hell. How did you live with that thing in here?"

"You ain' no garden yourse'f, Broom," Eldridge said. "You should take a smell of what your room is like sometime." Broom's face creased up like he was going to lose his temper. Then the sound came again and this time it was definitely a dog, kind of a half bark. Sounded like a dog barking in a coffee can. Pretty good-sized dog too, from the noise.

The dog growled and Eldridge felt the hair on the back of his neck rise. He could feel the vibrations from the growl rising up through the metal floor. It was like he was standing on the dog's rib cage. It was just under their feet and Eldridge caught himself looking down even though there was nothing there to see but old brown carpet. "Shoot," Broom said. "Did you hear that?"

Eldridge flicked the switch on the hunting lamp and the light came on. The beam was yellow. "Look kind of weak," Broom said. "Under there all the time the batt'ry probably gone bad."

"Jest cause it's so light up here," Eldridge said. "It'll be a lot brighter under the trailer."

"Huh," Broom said. "I expect that's so. I expect it's jest the day."

Eldridge kept flicking the switch on the light, testing it to see if it would get brighter or dimmer maybe. The yellow beam stayed the same. He went out to the living room, turned the tv off.

"You gonna take somethen under there with you?" Broom said. "I sure as hell wouldn' go under there without nothen to take the dog on."

"Take what," Eldridge said.

"I don' know. Sharp stick maybe."

"I'm jest gonna chase the dog out from under there. I ain' want to get in a fight with it."

"Well," Broom said. "But you wouldn' catch me under there without nothen. Never know what that dog could be like under there."

It was probably one of the strays that were always getting in the garbage or some dog that people from town had dumped off in the bushes Eldridge decided. Jest sick or strayed or something. Nothing to worry about.

He opened the door, stepped out onto the cinder block that was their front porch step. It shifted in the soft earth and he almost fell. "Son bitch," he said. It was a bright hot day and Eldridge had to shield his eyes from the sun.

"Wonder whose dog it might could be," Broom said. "People round here ought to take better care of their animals than let them run loose like that. Ought to be laws about that."

"Nobody's dog," Eldridge said. "It jest come here to die. That's when a dog goes in a dark place alone, when it wants to die."

He got down on his knees, peered into the crawl space. There was only one place to get under, right near the trailer door. The rest of the crawl space was closed off with tin. It looked like a pretty tight squeeze through the hole to Eldridge.

"I bet it's Seldomridge's dog," Broom said. "You know that big black bastard of a hound he got that's all the time getten in people's sheep. Somebody probably poisoned the son of a gun."

"Could be," Eldridge said.

The dirt under the trailer was black and damp, looked like dirt that would have worms up on the surface. There was no grass, just a lot of leaves piled up around the foundations of the place and around the pipes. Eldridge didn't think he'd ever seen so many pipes in a place before, couldn't think of what they would all be for. Septic tank he knew, for one. He felt his chest start to get tight.

"I hope it ain' got the rabies," Broom said. "I seen a dog that had the rabies once and it was an awful thing."

"It ain' got the rabies, Broom," Eldridge said.

"Got bit by a coon or a skunk and that sucker was plain crazy. Slobbers all over his mouth and blood runnen out his snout and down his chin. Walked all stiff-legged and hunchback and snapped at everthen that come too near. Like to bit some kids that was thowen stones at it."

Eldridge edged to the entrance into the crawl space. He tried to ignore Broom.

"Ended up by finally tearen his own guts out, he was that out of his head. Nothen else to bite on so he ripped out his own belly and bleeden and howlen while he buried his nose. Jesus was that somethen." He sounded excited.

"Was it," Eldridge said. He couldn't see anything under the trailer. The dog was way in the back.

"You bet," Broom said. "The county sheriff even come out to the trailer park where it was after a while but it was already dead by that time. Pulled out its own innards and the kids was hitten at it with rocks and sticks too. Big fat deputy put a round into it jest to make sure but it was dead as hell, flies crawlen on its tongue and all."

Broom paused to get his breath. Eldridge was glad of the quiet.

"You see it?" Broom said after a minute. "I'd hate for that to be Seldomridge's big old dog under there and stinken with the rabies. He'd bite on you sure as hell and then you'd have it too." He was standing on the cinder block by the door, rocking it back and forth in its place. It made a sucking sound in the dirt as he moved it.

Eldridge dropped to his stomach, belly-crawled a little ways in. He got his head under the trailer; his shoulders struck the tin on either side. He hunkered down, drew his shoulders in, got a little further. It was hard to raise the light in the narrow space. He couldn't get it up high enough to shine where he thought the dog should be. A leaf caught against his face and he could smell the rot on it. It smelled like it had been lying under the trailer for years.

"You see it yet?" Broom called from outside. His voice was muffled. Eldridge looked back, craned his head around as far as he could. He saw Broom's head, upside-down. All that Eldridge could see of the head was an outline, dark against the bright sunlight. He had never noticed before how odd-shaped Broom's head was, not like an egg or round but pressed in at the temples: rounded above and rounded below like a badly poured pancake. Broom's hair was hanging down and touching the ground.

"It ain' where I can see it," Eldridge said. "I'm gonna have to go in a little ways more."

"What?" Broom said. Eldridge didn't bother to say it again. He hauled himself forward with his elbows, throwing the Black and Decker's beam ahead of him. Even in the dark under the trailer the beam was yellow. It looked like Broom had been right in the first place about the battery. Outside, out from under the trailer, he could hear Broom yelling to him. He didn't try to catch the words.

The ground under him was cool and slick like he had thought it would feel. His knees were damp, and his forearms; the mud soaked through his pants, got into the creases of skin at his elbows. It was a tight place to be in and it made him nervous. He wasn't even thinking about the dog. He was all the way under the trailer. He pushed with his toes, tried to get some purchase to help him along but there wasn't enough grip there.

Eldridge couldn't believe the amount of stuff that there was under the trailer. Something that looked like the differential off an old four-wheel drive was near him on his left half-covered in leaves. He figured the people that had owned the trailer before him and Broom moved in had tossed it under there, why he had no idea. Next to that was a denim work glove looking like a dead man's hand sticking up out of the ground. Near the entrance was a little doll of a man that some kid had lost a long time before, what they called a Talking GI Joe. Eldridge knew if he pulled the string in its back the tiny record inside wouldn't make anything but gibberish.

A spider web that had stretched from one pipe to another touched his face, attached itself to him under his nose. He batted at it. "Son bitch," he said. The spider web floated up, got in his eyes. He kept his mouth tight shut for fear that it might get in there too. The thought of the cobweb in his mouth made him feel sick to his stomach. He shook his head, couldn't get rid of the thing. It seemed like it was floating in the air, more strands of it sticking to him all the time. He started to crawl back out toward the light, to get the spider web out of his eyes. He needed both hands free from crawling for that.

As he moved back his tee shirt pulled up under his arms, left his belly bare to the cool dirt. He gritted his teeth. He couldn't believe how much he wanted to make a noise. Broom wasn't saying anything anymore and Eldridge wished that he was, wished that he had left the tv on in the living room so that he could hear its noise through the floor. He figured he was about under the living room now.

When he twisted his head around he couldn't even see Broom's feet anymore. "Broom," he yelled. "Broom, where the hell you go?" His voice sounded loud bounced back to him from the pipes and the floor of the place, filled the crawl space. He shoved himself back some more, could feel the heat of the sun on the backs of his legs. Backwards was slow going but he only had a couple of more feet to be outside where he could stand up again. He blinked, trying to get rid of the spider web. There were bits of leaf or something caught in the strands and he could feel them against his face. His elbows dug into the ground as he pushed himself backwards.

Something moved at the far end of the trailer. He swung the light around as best he could, played it over the gray thing that he thought was the dog. No eyes, he couldn't see any eyes, couldn't tell if it was fur or not, no legs or tail.

He saw the dog. Like those trick pictures where at first you can't see what it is, just a bunch of light and dark places, and then you can, you can see the head of Jesus or the sea gull or whatever is there—that's the way that Eldridge saw the dog. It had risen up but there wasn't enough room for even it to stand straight-legged in the crawl space. It stood with its back against the floor of the trailer, legs bent, weaving a little. Its eyes were almost closed, swelled and full of pus; they shone half-moons of red light from the beam of Eldridge's flashlight.

It had the mange and not just a little mange either but the kind that can kill a dog. In places the thing looked like it had been peeled, the hair and skin taken off with a dull knife. Its chest was wide and deep but it was so starved its stomach curved up almost to its backbone like a racing dog's belly. It wasn't a racing dog though; it looked like one of those big German guard dogs. It growled, its wet lips peeled back from the gums and fluttering. The sound was deadened by the distance and by the bare dirt but it filled Eldridge's head.

He shoved himself back out from under the trailer. He kept the flashlight on the dog as he backed out. It didn't come any closer to him. It growled and growled and the growl swelled until it filled the whole crawl space like the sound of an organ. The dog was drooling and the drool was flecked white with pus.

Eldridge nicked his shoulder on the sharp edge of the tin at the entrance. He rolled over and stood up, dropping the flashlight. He rubbed at his eyes, got most of the spider web off his face. It stuck to his hands instead. "Broom," he called. He looked behind him, half expecting to see the mangy dog hauling itself out from under the trailer after him.

"Did you see it?" Broom said. He was sitting in the door, his feet on the cinder block. "You seen it under there didn' you?"

Eldridge nodded.

"Thought so," Broom said. "Was it Seldomridge's mutt like I said? You gonna go under there again so you can kill the sucker?"

"Ain' goen under there again," Eldridge said.

"Don' you worry, Eldridge," Broom said. "You'll get him next time. You jest got rattled a little is all. You'll be ok."

"You don' get it," Eldridge said. "That bastard can have it. I ain' goen in there after him again. You want to, you can get him out. I ain'." He thought about that dog with its lips pulled back. He wanted to get inside but he couldn't get past Broom sitting there in the doorway.

"Maybe he'll come out of there after a while on his own," Broom said. "Maybe he'll get hungry and jest come on out of there and we won' have to fool with him at all."

Eldridge pushed past Broom on into the trailer. "Shut that door," he said. He tried to get Broom out of the way so he could pull the door closed.

"He scared you that bad did he?" Broom said. He brushed Eldridge's hands off him. "Jesus Christ," he said, "what's wrong with you. Let me go."

Eldridge let go of him and he came on inside. "You don' want to pull on me like that," he said. "Man that's scared of a dog."

"You didn' see him," Eldridge said.

"Wouldn' of scared me if I did," Broom said.

"You didn' see him," Eldridge said again. "You go under there if you want. You shoot him if you want. But I'm tellen you I ain' goen in after that dog."

"Ain' nobody asken you to," Broom said. "We'll wait a while, see if he comes out by himse'f."

"If he don' then what?" Eldridge said.

"Then I'll figure a way to get him out," Broom said.

"With what?" Eldridge said. "A sharp stick?"

"Maybe so," Broom said. "Maybe that's how I'll do it." Eldridge laughed at him and Broom's face got red and angry.

* * *

Eldridge couldn't get to sleep that night for thinking about the dog. It hadn't come out that day at all and Broom hadn't gone in after it either. Eldridge was glad about that in a way. Still it meant he couldn't get to sleep for knowing the dog was probably not more than three or four feet from him, through the floor.

Once or twice he heard it moving around under the trailer, shifting so he could picture its mangy back brushing up against the floor and the pipes, see it pushing leaves around to make for a better bed. Always when he was about to get to sleep the dog would move around and moan and he would get to thinking about it again with its ugly animal-shine eyes and the pus in its drool. After a while he was afraid that he could smell the dog through the floor, smell it in the bed it was making for itself.

"Broom," he said, lying there. He knew Broom would hear him if he was awake. The walls in the trailer weren't much. He could hear Broom sometimes when he snored. He'd had to pound on the wall more than once to get Broom to roll over and shut up. "Broom," he said again.

He shifted over to his stomach, put his nose down in the pillow. He thought that if he could see down through the pillow and the mattress, straight through the floor, he would be looking right at the dog, at where the dog was asleep.

He wondered if the dog had dreams. He had seen dogs whine in their sleep, twitch their legs. "Chasen rabbits," was what he always thought to himself when he saw a dog twitch in its sleep. But this didn't sound like that when the dog under the trailer would move. This was bigger, shifting and bumping, and different. Eldridge didn't know what a sick dog would dream about when it had found the dark place where it wanted to die.

The dog whined and at first the whine was a high sound like a mosquito that is close to your ear. Then it was louder, a wail like some ghost, and Eldridge sat up in bed. "Goddam," he said. He listened to the dog howling. He would have sworn it was in the room with him it was so loud. He tossed his pillow away from him and it bounced off his dresser, landed on the floor. "I can' do this," he said. He got out of bed.

He crossed the room, walking softly. The noise the dog was making started to die away some but he kept walking, up on the balls of his feet. The padding under the carpet was going bad and it had broken up into lumps that moved when he stepped on them. Eldridge went into the bathroom that was down the hall from the smaller bedroom, took a leak. While he was in there he looked at himself in the mirror. He looked the same but tired. He wondered what time it was.

He flushed the toilet, thought about the dog lying near the pipe to the septic tank. The water rushing through would probably wake the dog up. Then it would really take to moving around down there. Eldridge didn't want to think about that.

On the way back to his room he opened Broom's door. He couldn't see Broom very well in the dark but he could hear him breathing. "You been hearen that dog, Broom?" he said. "Moven around under there."

"What the hell," Broom said, sitting up on his elbows in the bed. "What you doen, Eldridge?"

"Jest talken," Eldridge said. "I heard the dog still under there, it's keepen me awake. I thought you might of heard it."

"I was asleep till you woke me up," Broom said. He sounded angry. Eldridge didn't know if he had really been asleep or not. He reached up, grabbed the top of the doorway over his head, swung his weight on his arms. It felt good to stretch the muscles out.

"Well, I jest thought you might be up," Eldridge said. "We got to get that dog out from under there." Broom didn't say anything back. He was pretending to be asleep again. It made Eldridge mad that Broom wouldn't talk to him.

"I ain' goen to sleep in there anymore for a time," Eldridge said. "I want you to trade me rooms." Broom was still pretending to be asleep. "It's a bigger room," Eldridge said. "You know you always wanted it, Broom." He was tired standing there begging with Broom but he knew he wasn't going to be able to sleep in the other bedroom.

"Christ, Broom," he said. He didn't like the smell of Broom's place and it was too hot from having the window closed all the time. He hated to ask for it. Broom turned over, put his back to Eldridge. With both his hands he was holding tight to the pillow.

After a while more of standing there looking at Broom's back, Eldridge went and got the blanket off his bed. He had to look a little while in the dark to find where he had thrown the pillow. He took his stuff and spent the night on the floor in the living room.

*   *   *

"Hey Ed," Eldridge called. He and Broom stood out in the hot dust in front of Fat Ed Venner's house. There was an old Scout with no wheels sitting out in the yard. It had been up on jacks but one of them had collapsed so it was canted at an angle. Eldridge pointed at it. "You 'member when Ed used to have that thing out on the road?"

Broom shook his head. "Nope," he said. He had been quiet the whole morning.

It was a Sunday so they figured Fat Ed would probably be at home. Eldridge's back hurt. He had slept on it wrong on the hard floor. Broom kicked at the ground and the dry red clay scattered.

The screen door of Fat Ed's house swung open and a

woman stepped out onto the porch. She was thin, about forty years old, wiping her hands on a towel. Probably making Sunday supper Eldridge thought. She wore an old dress that the color had washed out of years before. Her figure made the dress look like it was filled with sticks. She stood on the porch, looking out at Broom and Eldridge. She had to squint against the sun to see them.

"Ed here?" Eldridge asked. The woman still didn't say anything. Broom kicked at the dirt again and Eldridge moved away from him to keep from getting the legs of his jeans dirty. Broom's boots were covered with dust.

"Around back," the woman said. Eldridge didn't move. "In the shed," she said. "You find him back there. You can always find him back there." She looked them up and down. "I want that you should ask him what it is he wants to work on them old useless junk for anyway." Broom didn't say anything. Eldridge cleared his throat.

"He all the time back there and putten together his worthless stuff and his daddy and me we got to walk into town if we want to go, ain' got a car between us that run. Now what kind of a son is that I want you should ask him."

"We jest come to borry somethen from him," Eldridge said.

"His uncle got him a job he could take anytime down to the garage at Organ Cave and he could easy do the work but he don' want it. He'd ruther hang around out back there and do nothen."

"I expect we'll go around and see him now," Eldridge said. The woman made him nervous. She was muttering to herself, lips moving but no sound coming out. She turned on him.

"And tell him not to be haven his yahoo friends comen around here on a Sunday."

"Biddy," Broom said but not loud enough that she could

hear him. Eldridge started around toward the back of the house. It wasn't so much, just a little frame house. One of the windows on the side had gotten busted out; it was patched up with cardboard and duct tape. The skinny woman stayed on the porch watching them go. Her eyes were hard and bright. Eldridge couldn't figure what made her so mad.

Fat Ed was standing outside the shed. There was a small motorcycle carburetor at his feet in a half-full bucket of gasoline. He didn't smile when he saw Broom and Eldridge. He was cleaning his nails with a jackknife, running the blade in deep under each nail trying to get at the grease and dirt there. "Yo Ed," Eldridge said.

Fat Ed nodded at them and his soft cheeks jiggled. He was sweating in the heat. He stood a hair under six feet tall, weighed maybe three hundred pounds. Eldridge couldn't figure a person letting himself get like that. Fat Ed moved like a Hereford steer, real slow and deliberate. He folded up the jackknife, stowed it in the pocket of his coveralls.

"Ain' seen you fellers in a while," he said.

"Hey Ed," Eldridge said. "What is it you worken on these days?" He pointed down at the carb in the bucket.

Ed grunted. "'Nother chopper," he said. "Boy was sellen a Vincent Black Shadow down to Heflin and didn' have the least idee what he had. I got it off him for next to nothen." Past Ed's wide body Eldridge could see that there were at least three motorcycles in the shed, one hanging by the wheels from a rack in the rafters, and parts for others, fenders and tires and throttle cable.

"We come to see could we borry a pistol, Fat Ed," Broom said like he was tired of waiting for Ed to finish talking. Ed's face turned red at the name and he pressed his lips together.

"Jesus, Broom," Eldridge said.

"What," Broom said. "He knows he's fat, don' he. What does he care if we know it."

"What is it you need it for?" Fat Ed said. He stood there and looked at them for a minute. They knew he had a bunch of pistols in his place, Colts and Mausers and Smith & Wessons. He even had a nickel-plated Llama revolver he'd shown to them one time. Fat Ed liked guns. They generally borrowed their rifles from him when they went deer hunting.

"We got to kill a dog," Eldridge said. "It's got in up under the trailer to die."

Fat Ed started for the back of the house and Eldridge had to walk fast to keep up with him. "Why'nt you jest let it die then?" Fat Ed said. "Then you won' have to borry nothen."

"'Cause who the hell knows when it's goen to die?" Broom said. He stood where he was, nearly shouting at Ed.

"We got to kill it today, Ed," Eldridge said. He figured Fat Ed wasn't going to lend them the pistol and that Broom had messed it up for them. "We figure it might have the rabies."

"Huh," Fat Ed said. "I guess I can see that. I guess maybe you better had kill the thing. What kind of pistol is it you want?"

"A big one," Broom said.

Eldridge looked at him and he shut up. "Pretty good-sized dog," Eldridge said. "Don' want to get in under there with some twenny-two and jest make the sucker mad."

"Yeah," Fat Ed said. "You gonna be the one to use it?"

"He ain'," Broom called out. "He ain' goen back in under there he says. Come out from under yesterday like to piss in his pants he's so scared."

"You shut up," Eldridge said, "'fore I come over there

and smack you one."

Broom spat. "Shoot," he said. He said something else under his breath.

"What's that," Eldridge said. Broom didn't say anything, stared at Eldridge and Fat Ed. His lips were moving.

"You can have it if it's you gonna use it," Fat Ed said. He looked at Broom. "I don' want that bastard to be the one."

"Shoot," Broom said again.

Eldridge nodded. "You bet, Ed," he said. "I'm gonna be the one."

Ed opened the door into the house. "That's all right then," he said. "You best not to come in the house. My ma don' like company on Sundays too much." He went inside and pulled the door to behind him.

Eldridge turned to Broom. "We about didn' get the gun 'cause of you," he said. "What do you want to talk like that for when we're asken to borry somethen?"

"Fat son bitch," Broom said. He put his hands in his pockets. "I don' know what we ever want to bother with him for anyhow."

"Hush up," Eldridge said.

"Don' you tell me. I'm tired of you tellen me all the time what to do, how to act. You and him, that fat hog, with all them motorcycles. What's he want with a motorcycle?"

"You want that dog there under our place till it decides to die?" Eldridge said.

"Who cares? You the one that's scared of it."

Fat Ed came back out of the house. He carried a flat black pistol in his right hand, a big one with checkered wooden grips. "Here you go," he said.

"Ho yeah," Broom said. "That'll do her." Fat Ed shot him a look, handed the pistol to Eldridge. It was heavy in his hand.

"That there's a Colt forty-five," he said. "You give that one a try. It's got a clip already in it."

"You bet," Eldridge said. "We'll see you after a while."

"Don' worry about it," Ed said. "I got to get back to work on that Vincent." He headed back into the shed, hunched next to a big bike that was heeled over on its kickstand in the middle of the shed. Eldridge watched Ed's hands working at the motor like small trained animals, tightening a bolt, cleaning a valve.

"Let's go," Eldridge said. He started back around the house toward the road. It was a couple of miles walk back to the trailer and the sun was hot.

"Fat bastard," Broom said. He trotted to keep up with Eldridge as they rounded the house. Broom kept his eyes on the pistol. Eldridge could tell he liked the way it looked. Around the other side of the house Fat Ed's mother was standing on the porch, her hand shading her eyes.

"You figure she been up there the whole time waiten on us?" Broom asked Eldridge. Eldridge shrugged.

"Did you tell him?" the woman called out to them. "He ain' got an ounce of sense, all the time tinkeren with them crazy bikes. I never did see nothen like it."

Broom puffed his lips out, made a shooting sound, laughed to himself. They kept walking. When they rounded the bend in the road about a quarter mile away, the woman was still out on the porch watching them.

* * *

When they got back to the trailer neither one of them went inside. They were both hot and sat down in the dirt of the yard. They looked at the trailer and at the entrance to the crawl space next to the door.

"You figure it's still under there?" Broom asked.

"I figure," Eldridge said. "Where would it go?"

They sat like that for a few minutes. A horsefly buzzed around Broom's head but he batted at it and it went away without biting him. Eldridge weighed the Colt in his hand, tipped it back and forth to test the balance. He worked the slide, saw the first oily brass round slip into the chamber. Fat Ed took good care of his guns.

"Get me the lamp, Broom," Eldridge said. Broom sat there.

"I ain' gonna get nothen," Broom said. "You such a big man you go get it."

Eldridge got up, went into the trailer. Fat Ed's gun swung heavy at his side. It was hot in the trailer, hotter than it was outside, and smelled bad. He wondered if the dog had died or something.

The lamp was in the living room and he got it, switched it on. The light was still pale and yellow. He walked outside again, kneeled down to go into the crawl space.

"Why don' you let me go," Broom said. "You been under and it scared you."

Eldridge didn't say anything back to him. He crawled in past the truck differential and the GI Joe. He looked at where the dog was, pointed the gun ahead of him. He wanted to get close so he could make sure to put it away with one shot. He shoved himself forward. The sweat from his palm slicked the wooden grip. He thumbed the hammer of the .45 back.

"Dog," he said. He couldn't figure why he was talking but the sound of his voice made him feel better. "I got to put you down," he said. The dog stirred in its bed of leaves and he shined the light down there on it.

The dog was off its feet, tried to struggle up but couldn't. It thrashed in the leaves, heaved its weight. It whined.

Eldridge pulled himself forward. He sighted down the blued barrel on the dog.

It managed to get on its feet but the hind legs were shaky. The dog wheeled to face Eldridge, showed its teeth at him. A loop of saliva hung from its long snout. It presented its chest like it wasn't afraid, like it wanted the bullet. Most animals could smell guns Eldridge knew.

Eldridge squeezed the trigger. The sound of the gun was deafening in the crawl space. Eldridge knew the shot went wild as soon as he let it go. The empty brass spanged off the bottom of the trailer and pattered across Eldridge's back. It felt warm through his shirt. He brought the pistol down again.

The dog hauled itself forward, scrabbling with its front paws. Its back legs were stiff, trailed out behind it. Through the ringing in his ears Eldridge could hear that it was growling, the same growl that he had heard in his bedroom up above.

He centered the sights of the pistol on the deep chest of the dog. The hair was missing there in whorls and patches; the skin was flaked and sore-looking. There was an old red leather collar around the dog's neck with a metal tag attached. The dog was only about a dozen feet from him.

He fired and the heavy round tore into the dog, ripped out from down around its hip. The slug snapped the dog's head around, knocked it off its feet and back about a yard. The dog raised its snout and tried to howl. It couldn't make anything but a noise like air rushing through a pipe. There was blood on its nose and teeth. It moved its front paws in the dirt, lying on its side.

"Got you," Eldridge said. He moved up to where the dog lay on its side in the dirt, panting like almost any dog might on a hot day trying to pull some cool out of the hot still air. The skinny rib cage went in and out, in and out. The bullet had caved in the chest cavity and the dog was about dead.

Eldridge looked at the dog's eyes and they were flat and lifeless as mud puddles. There was mucus caked in the corners of its eyes and the dog blinked, trying to clear them. It opened its jaws wide and puked blood onto the cool dark floor of the crawl space.

Eldridge held the light close to the dog's head. He looked at the tag on the red leather collar but the metal was tarnished and he couldn't read what was written there. The collar was old and the leather was cracked. While he was trying to make out what was engraved on the collar the dog flopped once. It closed its eyes and he couldn't hear the breath pumping into its shattered lungs anymore.

*   *   *

Eldridge watched a big black digger beetle, big as the first joint of his thumb, crawl across clumps of rotted leaves and dirt toward the dog. He figured the dog's blood had brought it. The smell of the blood was strong, like sulfur, there under the trailer.

The beetle's shell was shiny and polished-looking, like the finish on a new car. The bug went past the toes of Eldridge's boots and he thought about squashing it. When he pointed the flashlight at it, the beetle hurried in under the dog's body. "Christ Amighty," Eldridge said.

The dog was in a strange position, half on its back, one front leg sticking up in the air. Its thick gray tongue was pushed out of its mouth, looked dry. Eldridge put the pistol on the damp ground next to him. He felt tired.

He clicked the flashlight off. In the dark the dog was just a hump. He closed his eyes. "Didn' have nobody in the world to take up for you, did you," he said. If they left the dog under the trailer, he knew the digger beetles would come and bury it, lots more than just the one he had seen.

He could hear Broom shouting his name out from under the trailer. After a while of shouting he stuck his head into the crawl space. His face was a dark patch, hard to see framed against the bright sunlight. "Yo Eldridge," he shouted. He squinted his eyes but Eldridge figured he couldn't see anything without the hunting lamp. Eldridge liked it that Broom couldn't see him.

"Crazy son bitch," Broom said when Eldridge didn't answer. He disappeared back outside and Eldridge heard him go into the trailer. Broom stomped on the floor not far above Eldridge's head. Eldridge closed his eyes. After a minute, he heard the tv in the living room come on. It sounded like Broom had turned it up very loud. Eldridge sighed and shook his head, listening to Broom's footsteps cross and recross the living room of the trailer.

Pit

B runty thought that Paxco was going for a gun, so he
went into his jacket and jerked out the thin-bladed
fillet knife, stuck it right into Paxco's chest. Paxco folded
up against the plywood barrier around the dog pit, cough-
ing blood.

The dogs in the pit, the little spitz and the big black
mutt, just kept on going at it, with the slow mutt taking
most of the damage. The spitz was awful quick and a better
fighter than his size might make you think. He was out
of King Generator up in Pocahontas County, and King
Generator was a dog that was born to fight.

The two motorcycle crazies and the out-of-town high
roller just stood and watched the whole thing happen. The
high roller had expected some excitement but he hadn't
figured on anything like this. He hadn't figured on seeing
the pit owner get knife-murdered during the fights. He
stood back against the wall of the barn while Paxco died.

Brunty tried to pull the knife out of Paxco's chest but it
was stuck on a rib and wouldn't come. He was about
crying, watching blood come out of Paxco's mouth. The

fillet knife had cost Brunty two and a half bucks at the True Value in town. He had started carrying it for protection a couple of months earlier, when Paxco's boys had threatened to break his fingers for not paying Paxco what he owed, and the first time he ever pulled it was when he shoved it into Paxco's lung.

The handle of the knife was orange so you could see it if you dropped it in the dark. It looked strange to Brunty, the day-glo handle, designed to float in the water, the fisherman's friend, sticking out of Paxco. It looked like a lever you might pull to start some machine going.

"Christ Amighty," Paxco said to Brunty. His fingers feathered the butt of his police .38 but he wasn't strong enough to pull it out of its holster so he could kill Brunty. He felt the breath going out of him. He felt it going out through the hole that Brunty had made in his chest, and he wanted to smoke Brunty for that.

Paxco had done a lot of things in his life that he figured were bad enough he should die for them, if you were a Christian that believed in such things. Divine retribution. Still, he was surprised to get it from a little bastard like Brunty.

He tried again to pull the gun out of the leather shoulder holster but just dropped it down in the sawdust next to his leg. It was a flat black revolver with fancy rubberized Pachmayr grips, a gun like a quick-draw artist might have. Paxco held his hands up in front of him, tried to close them but couldn't. They felt like they were swelling.

Brunty leaned close over Paxco, trying to figure out what to do about the knife. He felt stupid and slow, knew he had to get out of there quick. It was just luck that none of Paxco's boys were there that evening, just good luck that Brunty wasn't spread out dead on the floor already.

Paxco had three big boys that worked for him, collecting

money and busting heads, just generally keeping the peace. They all three carried cut-down shotguns that they called *lupos*, which was a name they had heard in some movie about the Mafia. They would have killed Brunty without thinking twice about it, dumped his body in a lime pit up on the mountain and been done with it. They had done things just like it and worse before.

"Kiss my ass, Brunty," Paxco said, and shivered. Brunty looked at him, saw the spirit leave out of his body. It was like watching a light go out in somebody else's house.

Paxco's hands rested in his lap, folded one over the other, very white and clean-looking. Paxco didn't have any dirt under his fingernails, which were neat and trimmed. He had always been careful about how his hands looked. Brunty watched the eyelids close down over Paxco's dead empty eyes.

The dogs on the other side of the barrier quit their fighting. For a minute Brunty thought it was because they sensed Paxco's passing. He was struck by that, the fact that dogs could tell when a man died and take note of it, stop what they were doing.

When he looked, he saw that the big black mutt had killed the fast little spitz in spite of the predictions. The spitz had taken an ear off of the mutt. The ear lay in the middle of the pit, looking dull and chewed and wrinkled. Brunty had seen nights when there were four or five ears left in the sawdust of the pit, lying there like winter leaves. The black dog had its square head down in the open belly of the spitz. Its thick bald tail whipped from side to side.

"You are in for a world of hurt," one of the motorcycle crazies said to Brunty. He was a fat man with a little goat beard that he held together with a rubber band. He wore a long black raincoat. His partner had a pair of little round dark glasses which made him look like he was blind.

Brunty snatched up the heavy revolver next to Paxco's body, pointed it to cover the two men. "Stay still and just don't move at all," Brunty said. He kept the .38 mainly on the guy with the beard. The black raincoat looked like a good place to keep a piece. He didn't want any more surprises.

The high roller was still in his corner. He couldn't take his eyes off of Paxco. He was surprised at how bright the blood was on Paxco's shirt. He was a candidate for state senate and didn't think this kind of thing would be good for his campaign. He couldn't be sure though. Sometimes it was hard to tell what the voters would get behind.

It took Brunty a couple of tries to thumb back the hammer on the revolver. You're gonna have to do them too, he kept hearing in his head. They seen you put steel to Paxco. It was like a nightmare, that he was going to have to kill three more people just because he had killed Paxco. Brunty was panicked. He couldn't think of a way around it.

The guy with the glasses laughed. "You'd best to get out of here quick, man. You got some trouble coming down." He gestured at Paxco, who looked like he was sleeping, except for the blood and the orange handle of the knife. "You got worst enemies than us," the guy said. Brunty thought of the three bruisers with the double-barreled *lupos*. He didn't know where they were but it was a bet they wouldn't be gone all night. The stink from the dead dog's guts—or maybe it was Paxco—was getting to him.

"Nobody leave here for ten minutes after I go," he said. The motorcycle riders just looked at him. They didn't care what he said. The high roller looked like he was crying. Seeing that made Brunty feel strong for a second, knowing he could make a man cry. "I could kill you," he told them. "I could of killed all of you but I didn't." Keeping the revolver on them, he backed out of the barn.

Outside in the cool early morning air, Brunty looked
around for where he had parked his car. The rusted-out
Dodge Dart was where he had left it, near the door. Two
other guys, young kids from the county, sat in the back
of an old Ford pickup, waiting for their time in the pit.
They didn't know what had happened inside, stared at
Brunty with his cocked revolver.

They had their dog chained to the bumper of the truck.
It was just a block-headed yellow hound with big paws
and a long whip tail. Brunty remembered a dog like that.
He remembered drinking from a jar, dragging on a butt,
waiting for a dog like that to circle rabbits around to him.
That memory was strong in Brunty.

He paused as he was getting into the Dodge. "Get out
of here," he said to the kids. "You don't want to be here."
They just looked at him. They didn't know about anything
bad. They had heard about the high roller and his money
and they wanted their chance at some of it.

Brunty uncocked the revolver, tucked it inside his jacket
where he had kept the fillet knife. He started the Dodge,
pulled around Paxco's old dented Continental and the Har-
ley hogs the motorcycle boys had come in on. The block-
headed dog yelped and scrambled under the truck, pelted
by gravel from Brunty's spinning tires. The two kids put
their arms across their faces to keep from getting cut by
the rocks as Brunty pulled out of the lot.

* * *

Inside the barn, the two motorcycle crazies stuck around
just long enough to pull out their flick knives and take all
the money off the high roller. They also made him swear
to tell the police and Paxco's shooters that it was Brunty
who killed Paxco, and not them. They knew the assump-

tions that people make about other folks that ride motorcycles, and they wanted to be sure they were protected.

They left the one-eared black dog behind only with re-
gret. When they left he was pulling the heart out of the
little spitz. They would have taken him if they could have
figured a way to get him on one of the bikes without falling
off. They liked his style, and there was no telling how
much a dog that could kill a son out of King Generator
was worth.

* * *

Brunty pulled up in front of Sister Sue's. Sister Sue was
a woman that ran a place up in the hills of Pocahontas,
and Brunty figured she would put him up for a while,
only until he worked out what he could do, where he
could go. It was sure as hell he could not go home again,
not after he had murdered Paxco.

"Yo Sue," he called as he got out of the Dodge. Sister
Sue's was a blue two-story house about a hundred yards
off the mountain road. It had taken Brunty forty-five minutes to get up there. The sun was rising, and a cool breeze
blew through the pine trees that surrounded the place. A
couple of ragged yellow-colored chickens scratched and
pecked in a patch of bare dirt in front of the porch.

"Sister Sue," Brunty yelled at the house. The front door
opened and she stepped out onto the porch. She was a
tall, handsome woman with a nose that had been broken
some years ago. She pulled her bathrobe tight around her,
looked at Brunty like she didn't know who he was.

"It's Brunty," he said to her. Suddenly he wasn't sure
whether Sister Sue's was the place to be. He didn't think
she owed any love to Paxco, but it was hard to tell. A lot
of things got confused when you stuck a knife into the

chest of a man like Paxco.

"Hey Brunty," she said. "You got any money?"

Brunty looked down. "Got a lot of trouble, Sue," he said. "Figured I might could put up here for a little."

Sister Sue laughed at him. It was the kind of laugh she gave men just before she told them to get out. She liked Brunty pretty well because he was a small man and fairly clean and seldom a wicked or brutal drunk. "How come you always come to me when you got no money," she said to him. "You think I can eat trouble?"

"I busted caps on Paxco," Brunty said. He figured it was best to come right out with it. No use to cover anything up.

Sue snorted. "Bullshit," she said. "How come you ain't dead then?"

"I swear to God," Brunty said. "His boys was out running shine or something is why they didn't kill me. I run a knife right through his chest. He sat down and spit blood and then he died."

Sue stood and looked at Brunty for a couple of minutes. The bathrobe she had on was thin and he could see the solid flesh of her legs through the material. Her hair was long and the dull copper color of an old penny. She had it tied behind her neck with a broad black ribbon.

"You sure do look good, Sister Sue," he said.

"I never been flattered by a man that was dead and still walking around," Sister Sue said. She stepped to one side, motioned for him to come up on the porch. "I guess you best to come on inside."

Brunty followed her into the old house, which smelled to him like eggs over easy, like clean bedclothes. Sister Sue led him into the kitchen, sat him down at the table. There was a red-and-white-check plastic tablecloth on it. He rested his arms on the table, looked around at the enamel-white stove, refrigerator, sink. It didn't seem to him like this could be the same world where he had killed Paxco. He couldn't see this place with his blood spilled all over the clean white appliances. He relaxed a little.

"You ought not to of called me a dead man," he said to Sue. It was the first time this thought had occurred to him, that he should be insulted by her calling him that. She had her back to him, putting together an egg sandwich for him. She knew he liked an egg sandwich when he was hungry.

"I ain't dead yet," he said to her. He took the plate with the sandwich on it out of her hands. He felt more like eating now. He hadn't been sure he wanted to eat before, but with the sandwich in front of him he felt like he could put something down after all.

"I guess not," she said, looking at him. "But what kind of future you figure you got, the man that put the knife into Paxco?"

"I might do okay," he said. He took a bite of the sandwich and it tasted good to him. He figured that a man that had an appetite was a man that could go on living for a while. "There's more places than just around here. I could take the Dodge and go up to Pennsylvania, Maryland maybe. Lots of places a man could go."

"What would make you do a thing like stabbing Paxco? You know they got to kill you for trying something like that," she said. "You never did a thing like that before that I knew of."

He looked at her, held his right hand up in front of him. He stared at it like it was the cause of all his troubles. "I went up to the pit to ask him for some more time," he said. Sue shook her head at him.

"He moves like he's going for his gun, don't want to

talk to me but just wants to waste me on the spot. So I stuck him. It was the fastest thing I ever done, like I didn't do it at all. I swear, it was like somebody else just jumped into my skin and done it for me."

"You crazy bastard, Brunty," she said to him. He mopped his plate with the crust of the sandwich. "They'll catch up to you," she said.

"Maybe," he said. "I figure."

"So how do you figure to keep alive when they do?" she said. "Them three boys with the *lupos* will cut you to pieces."

He thought about that. It was a good question. He reached inside his jacket, pulled out the .38 with the Pachmayr grips. He put it down on the table in front of him. It looked funny, the flat black steel next to the plate with egg on it. He picked it up again, hefted it. The gun had a good balance to it. "I took this off of Paxco," he said.

Sister Sue looked at Brunty sitting at her table with the revolver in his hand, playing with it like he was some kid. "Didn't seem to benefit him overmuch," she said. She picked the plate up from in front of him, put it in the sink so it could soak clean.

*   *   *

Brunty was in Sister Sue's bed when Paxco came to him. He was relaxing on the clean cool sheets, stripped down to his shorts. He was thinking about Sister Sue, wondering if she was going to sleep with him. He wanted that a lot, for Sue to walk into the room and shed that bathrobe she was in. He figured that would be a good way to spend the last of his time in the area. He had made love to Sue before and she was good at it. Better than he was. He could hear her cleaning up in the kitchen downstairs.

As he was thinking this, Paxco came into the room and sat down on the edge of the bed. He sat down in a patch of light that came through the blue curtains on the window. He turned to look at Brunty lying there in the comfortable bed, and there was blood on his lips and down his chin. The blood was dark and dried.

"Hey Brunty," Paxco said. When he spoke Brunty could see that there was blood on his teeth too. He was a mess of blood.

"Don't I know it," Paxco said. He nodded at Brunty. "I never would of knowed I had this much inside me. Something about busting a lung though is what I understand. When you get into a lung, you get a lot of blood." He laughed. The orange knife handle coming out of his chest bobbed up and down when he laughed like that, and Brunty wished he wouldn't.

"You got a piece of the heart too," Paxco said. He didn't sound angry or anything. Paxco had always been a calm character. That had been a big part of his success in the rackets, that he never got mad on the outside, never let his emotion slow him down. Brunty could tell that he hadn't died in terror.

He couldn't see through Paxco or anything. The man wasn't like a ghost at all. He listened and he could still hear Sue in the kitchen down below. He wanted to call out to her, scream out that Paxco was in here with him. He thought maybe Paxco had come to kill him. Paxco was still wearing his leather holster. It hung empty under his armpit.

"You ain't alive, are you," he said to Paxco. His voice came out small and weak, and he knew there was no way that Sister Sue would hear him.

"Christ," Paxco said. He sounded exasperated. He put his hand on Brunty's knee. Brunty could feel the weight of Paxco's hand on his knee through the sheet. He could feel the grip in the hand. It felt like he figured Paxco's hand would of felt, if Paxco had ever touched him like this when he was alive. "You ain't very smart, Brunty," Paxco said. "Plus you are just about dead."

"Who's going to kill me, Paxco?" Brunty said. "You going to do it?"

"You know who," Paxco said. "They can't let you go. They can't afford to. Folks would start to figure maybe they could get away with something too."

Brunty reached around next to him, put his hand on the night table for the revolver. He couldn't find the gun, knocked the little lamp off the table onto the floor. It didn't bust when it hit the floor, rolled around for a couple of seconds.

"You know," Paxco said, "the man that owns old King Generator lives a couple miles from here." He frowned. "That whelp wasn't worth too much was he?"

"I guess not," Brunty said. "I didn't have nothing to bet on him anyway."

"You could go see that guy," Paxco said. "Tell him his pup got eat up by some mongrel. But you ain't got the time." He smiled. Brunty didn't have anything to say.

"Anyhow," Paxco said, "I just wanted to come and see you. See the man that killed me." He patted Brunty's knee, studied his face for a couple of seconds. "I can't believe it was a little son of gun like you that did it. You come at me so fast I didn't know what was going on."

"Were you going for the .38?" Brunty asked.

"Hell yes," Paxco said, and he smiled. "I was going to put a couple through your forehead, just because I didn't like you. I would of cooked you if you hadn't of got to me first." He stood up from the bed.

"That's good then," Brunty said. He hoped Paxco was

going. He couldn't stand to look at that knife handle anymore.

"Or maybe I was just going to scratch myself," Paxco said. His voice was mean. "Or grab a cigarette. You ain't got the time to find out, Brunty."

On his way out, Paxco kicked his foot against the little table lamp. "You ought to be more careful, Brunty," he said. Paxco seemed to find that pretty funny. Brunty couldn't see the humor in it.

Paxco walked out of the room. Brunty closed his eyes. Outside the window a woodpecker drilled a hole into a hard old oak. He had read somewhere that a woodpecker hits a tree with its head at nearly a hundred miles an hour, over and over again, half a dozen times a second. He didn't see how it was possible for something to live through that kind of punishment.

"Sue," he called out. His voice was still weak. He had forgotten about having sex with her. He wanted to ask her about Paxco. He wanted to see what she thought about him coming in like that. He wanted to see if she thought that such a thing was able to happen. He kept his eyes closed so he couldn't see the patch of light on the bedspread where Paxco had been sitting.

* * *

Sister Sue woke Brunty up when it got dark outside. She put the lamp back on the table and turned it on before she shook his shoulder. When he looked at her she handed him a newspaper. "Take a look at that," she said. "I thought you might want to see it."

Brunty spread the paper out on his lap. *"Local Man Murdered"* was a headline on the front page. They had a picture of Paxco next to the column of newsprint, Paxco in a leather jacket sitting on the hood of his Continental. The front page told about him, his record and running the dog pit and all. The story was continued further back in the paper, and Brunty turned to the page.

There was an old picture of himself as a volunteer fireman. He looked like a kid with the big fire helmet sitting on his head. He figured they had got the photo from his ex-wife. It was funny that she still had a picture of him after all that time. He had enjoyed the fires he had helped to fight. That had been some excitement.

"You didn't tell me about no motorcycle gang," Sue said. "They don't figure it was just you killed Paxco. They think them motorcycle boys was in it too." There was a picture of the high roller on the page with Brunty's. He had told a story that got Brunty and the motorcycle crazies all mixed up in the killing. Brunty scanned the page for something about the two kids and their yellow dog, but there was nothing. That meant they had got away from it. He was glad of that.

He read in the paper where the cops had killed the one-eared mongrel. They said it was too vicious to do anything with. The rest of the dogs, the ones out back of the barn in the wire hutches, were at the pound. Brunty wondered what Paxco would think of that, his dogs dead or heading to the gas chamber.

"Paxco was in here a while ago," he said to Sister Sue. She didn't say anything back. He was really interested in how she felt about it. "I wanted to yell out for you but I couldn't," he said.

Sue stepped back away from Brunty, toward the door. There was something funny about the way she looked at him. "We got to move your car," she said. "Setting out in front like that, somebody is bound to see it." She was gone out the door before Brunty even realized what was going on. The three shooters had sent Sister Sue in to see if she would try to tip him off, to see if they had to kill her too. They were waiting just outside in the hall.

He was scrambling around on the night table for the revolver when the first of them shot him. The gun wasn't anywhere that he could see it. In his rush to find it, he knocked the lamp off the bedside table again, and this time the bulb busted on the floor.

The three boys with the double-barreled *lupos* blew him out of bed and onto the floor. The heavy shot cut tight patterns in the sheets. They were close enough that powder burned the weave black.

Brunty rolled across the floor and the three men came on across the room, fired into his body again. Buckshot tore up the board floor of the place. The last thing he knew was that his legs were tangled in the sheets and that he had to get them loose if he wanted to run. He died trying to get his legs out of the sheets.

"He ain't near as tall as I thought from his picture," one of the boys said, poking at the body with his 12 gauge. Out in the hall, Sister Sue listened to them and felt sad and sick, in spite of the fact that she had managed to save herself from the ugly situation that she was in.

* * *

The killers brought Brunty's corpse out of the house wrapped in the bedsheets. He was a mess to carry and they were pretty much disgusted with the job. "We cleaned his clock," one of the boys said. He was glad to see Brunty dead. He had thought a lot of Paxco.

They dumped the body in the trunk of Brunty's own Dodge. The motorcycle crazy with the little black glasses was already in there, as dead as Brunty. They figured to drive the car off a cliff further up in the mountains. It was a good six-hundred-foot wooded drop into a narrow gorge that they knew about. It would probably be months or years before some hiker tripped across the old car and the dead bodies.

They figured to get the other motorcycle rider if they could find him. Somebody would give him up to them after a while, like Sue had given them Brunty.

"This's okay because it's vengeance, but the next one's got to be neater," the biggest of the killers said. "We got to be businesslike about this stuff." He wiped his hands on a clean part of the sheet, wiped them again on his jeans. The other two nodded.

"Did you hear what he said about Paxco?" one of the other killers asked.

"Off his nut," the biggest one said. "Paxco's stiff as a poker." The big one was in charge now. He figured that maybe Paxco had got what was coming to him. He figured that with him running things they all stood to do a lot better. He was grateful to the corpse in the trunk of the Dodge, in a strange way.

"You boys have killed a lot of people," Sister Sue said from the porch of her house. The biggest boy looked at her as he stepped into the Dodge to drive it up the mountain, and his eyes on her made her feel cold.

"We didn't kill anybody that didn't need killing," he said to her. He started the Dodge, guided it down her driveway. The other two shooters followed a safe distance behind him and the two dead men, stayed about five car lengths back, driving Paxco's big old Continental up the mountain.

Fat Tuesday

"Fat Tuesday," the whole family cried, and Jason Goodell grinned at them all before he emptied out the burlap sack into the boiling water. All afternoon Jason had waited for the water in the big iron pot to boil; he'd watched that sack, full of crawdads, clicking and moving and crackling next to the pot. He'd driven all the way around to the other side of Lake Pontchartrain to get the crawdads, to a place he knew had the best live 'dads in Louisiana. Now the water was hot, and it was time to eat.

Jason shook the sack, and the crawdads fell into the water, ten and fifteen at a time, then more as he shook the sack harder. They clung to each other with their small claws, forming chains of crawdads, pulling each other in. A few held on to the burlap, but they were quickly brushed loose by Sara Goodell, Jason's wife. Her hair hung loose; her face was red from the heat of the fire.

"Goddam, look at them," said Cousin Mobrey Davis, clapping his thick hands together in front of him. Whenever one of the crawdads missed the pot, tried to

scuttle away, he would bend and scoop it up in his fist.
"Into the swimmin' hole," he'd say, and toss it into the
pot. Jason liked Mobrey, the middle-aged bachelor man,
with his scuffed boots and his eye for the girls.

Jason stood back from the pot to let the crawdads boil.
He folded his hands over his fat stomach, smiled as he
watched the family gather around the water.

All afternoon Jason's family—his aunt, Minnie Imogen,
and some old lady with her that Jason didn't know; his
seventeen-year-old niece Verna that had come with the
two old ladies; all the people on Sara's side of the family,
from over in Mississip—all of them had petted the sack,
and peeped into it, listened to the creaking of the shells
of the crawdads, the scraping of their claws. Twenty
pounds of crawdads. They'd be finished cooking pretty
soon.

Sara came up to Jason, put her lips next to his ear.
"There's something up with Bud Semples," she said. "He's
been acting queer, not talking. Minnie Imogen declares
she thinks he's crazy." Bud Semples was Jason's second
cousin, just about Jason's age, forty or thereabouts, Jason
wasn't sure exactly.

"Where's he at?" Jason said.

"Up on the porch," Sara said. "Mebbe you better see
about him."

"Yuh," said Jason. He unfolded his hands, turned and
went onto the screen porch of the house.

Bud sat on the porch in one of Jason's plastic lawn chairs.
He held a can of Black Label beer in one hand, a Camel
in the other. He was losing his hair, Jason noticed. The
look of high piss-off on Bud's face made Jason pause a
second before speaking.

"Yo, Bud," he said. Bud didn't even look at him, just
took a drag on his butt, stared at the pot of water out in

the yard. "Something wrong? Why ain't you out there with the rest?"

"I'm okay," Bud said.

"Sure," Jason said. "Everybody wants to see you, though. Come on out."

"Naw," Bud said. He shook his beer can, set it down on the porch floor. "I'll stay here a while."

Jason crouched next to Bud's chair. His knees popped, and he grunted with the effort. "You gotta come out," Jason said. "It's just about time to eat. Gotta eat."

Bud was quiet so long that Jason thought he wasn't going to answer. Jason listened to the rest of the family out on the lawn, heard Mobrey Davis pronounce the crawdads just about perfect, heard young Verna giggle. "You all coming?" Sara called. He was about to speak again when Bud looked up.

"You want me to eat them . . . them bugs?" he said. "Nawsir," he said. "I don't think so."

Jason stared at him. Bud was shaking his head. "I'm gonna go in and get me another beer," Bud said. "That's what I need." He stood, went into the house. All the doors and windows of the place were open, and the smell of cooking crawdads filled the air, a light, salt smell.

"Jase," Sara called, and Jason went back out and joined the family around the crawdad pot. "Don't they smell good," young Verna said.

"You gonna let 'em boil too long," Minnie Imogen said.

"You want to watch that," said the other old woman, the one Jason didn't know. "They ain't very good you let 'em set in the water too much."

Cousin Mobrey Davis patted Jason on the back. "You gonna eat you some crawdads, I bet," he said. "Big boy like you's bound to put some of them 'daddies down."

"Yuh," said Jason. He looked into the pot. The shells

of the crawdads were red. "Yuh," he said. "Gonna put some down."

*   *   *

Jason ladled the steaming crawdads out onto the paper plates the family held, ladleful after ladleful of them, pounds and pounds of them. "Here you go," he said to everyone in the family as they passed in front of him, and put enough crawdads on each plate to near bend it in half. "Take you some more," he'd say, "there's plenty for every-body."

"Oowee, they're hot," said Cousin Mobrey Davis, tossing one back and forth between his hands. "Watch out now, they'll burn your tongue." He leaned over Verna, wedged himself between her and Minnie Imogen. Verna looked at him with big eyes. "You take care, honey, they'll scald you," he said.

He cracked one open, pulled out the soft meat, tossed it into his mouth. "Oh yes," he said, "now that's good." Minnie Imogen grasped Verna's arm.

"You come and sit with me and Estelle," she said.

"I'll show you how to eat those crawdads," said Cousin Mobrey Davis. Minnie Imogen looked at him. "I'll keep you company," he said. He laughed. Minnie Imogen scowled.

*   *   *

"This is a good one," Jason said to Sara. He looked around him, at all the family spread around on the grass, with their paper plates and their ice chests full of Carling Black Label. He looked into the pot, saw that most of the crawdads were gone. "A good one," he said.

"Sure is, Jase," said Sara. She snapped the tail of a craw-dad, split the scaly skin and pulled the meat out. Jason watched her put the morsel in her mouth, bite into it with her white, even teeth. She tossed the shell of the crawdad into a black Hefty bag next to her.

"I wonder 'bout Bud, though," Jason said. Sara shook her head, broke the tail off another crawdad, washed the meat down with a swig of beer. Jason took the ladle and spooned a few crawdads onto a fresh paper plate. The plate went limp with the heat and wetness of them, so he curled it in his hand. "Think I'll try to go find him," he said. Sara nodded, cracked another crawdad.

Cousin Mobrey Davis put a hand on Jason's ankle as he went past, on his way into the house. "Where you headed, Jase?" he said. "You ain't done with the crawdads yet, are you?" He grinned at Verna, who was struggling with the shell of one. Her pretty little face was screwed up in a grimace. She'd spilled McIlhenny tabasco on her blouse. Jason couldn't see Minnie Imogen anywhere nearby, figured that suited Mobrey Davis just fine.

"Looking for Bud," Jason said. "You seen him?"

"Naw," said Cousin Mobrey Davis. He turned back to the girl, took the crawdad from her. "Here, honey, you want to let me do that for you." She smiled.

Jason went into the house. He met Minnie Imogen and the other old lady on their way out. Minnie Imogen had an open bottle of creole sauce, the hot kind they make over in New Iberia, in one hand.

"Bud in there?" he asked her.

She ignored him, looked past his shoulder. "That damn Mobrey Davis," she said. The other old lady shook her head in agreement.

*   *   *

Jason found Bud sitting in the tv room just off the front parlor. There were four or five beer cans standing around his chair. The tv was on to some station out of New Orleans, across the lake. The picture came in pretty well. On the screen, an old man sat in a straight-back chair on a bare stage, playing the guitar. Bud had the sound down, so Jason didn't know what the old guy was playing. His skinny hands moved slowly, carefully on the steel strings of the guitar.

"Ho," Jason said, and heaved himself into one of the rattan chairs. It creaked, and he remembered that Sara had told him to sit more slowly. "You'll bust one of them chairs flopping down like that," she'd said. "Then where'll you be?"

"On my ass," he'd said, and they'd both laughed.

Bud didn't look at him. Jason held out a greasy plate of crawdads to him. It was cool now, and a little juice leaked onto the floor of the tv room. "Brought you in some 'dads," Jason said. Still Bud didn't take his eyes off the guitar player.

"Yo, Bud," Jason said. "Everything all right?"

"Sure," Bud said.

Jason leaned forward, held out the plate. "Here you go," he said.

Bud pushed at his arm. "Get those out of here, will you," he said.

"They're good," said Jason. "Hell yes, you gotta have some, Bud. It's Fat Tuesday." Again he pushed the plate forward, closer to Bud's face this time.

"No," Bud said. He struck Jason's arm, and the plate collapsed. The crawdads spilled across the floor. One of them skidded under Jason's chair. Neither of the men moved.

"Now look what you done," Jason said.

"Dammit," said Bud. He got out of the chair, kneeled right on a crawdad. It crunched, soaked Bud's knee. He stood quickly, brushed at the leg of his pants. "Ugh," he said. One of the little claws refused to be brushed off, stuck to the material. He batted at it, shook the leg. Jason leaned over and picked it off for him.

Bud stepped away, kicked over one of the beer cans. "Making a mess," he said under his breath.

"You drunk?" Jason asked.

"So what about it?" Bud said. "Thought it was Fat Tuesday. Thought a man could get drunk on Fat Tuesday if he wanted."

"A man can, I guess," Jason said. He stood, moved to go. "Just wanted to bring you in some crawdads," he said.

"I'm sorry, Jase," Bud said. "I just had too much."

"Yuh," Jason said. "You better slow down."

The two men sat for a while, watching the old guitar player on tv. His mouth moved; he was singing along with the guitar now.

"You 'member how we used to get with the Bourbon Street girls in the city?" Bud said. "You 'member that one old girl, Shirleen? She sure did take to you."

"Hmm," said Jason.

"We used to have us a pretty good time," said Bud. "With them girls, them strippers. There's worse things than getting naked with a couple whores, Jase."

"I figure so," said Jason. "That was a while ago, Bud. I got a wife." The old man was leaving the stage on tv now. A couple of boys were helping to hold him upright as he walked.

"Yeah," said Bud. "But it's a lot of things. The heat. I 'member we used to like the heat. Used to like to go into Orleans when it was real hot, when the asphalt was soft as clay."

"I don't like the heat," said Jason. "It wears me out."

"That's what I mean," said Bud, "that's just what I'm talking about. I don't like the heat either. Not anymore."

He picked up the beer can he'd kicked over, swirled it around to see if there was anything left in it. He looked at the crawdads on the floor, picked one up, looked at it.

"Leave 'em," Jason said.

"Huh?"

"Leave 'em," Jason said again. "Sara'll get 'em later."

Bud flicked the little red body into the trash can next to his chair.

"Best I get back out to the family," Jason said. "They'll be wondering where I am."

"Jase?" Bud said. Jason waited.

"You ever think how we're getting old? You ever think about dying?"

Jason shifted his weight, shook his head. "You ain't old," he said. "What are you, forty, forty-two?"

Bud went on. "You ever think how it's gonna be when you feel that pain up your left arm, Jase? Or when the doc gives you that look and tells you it's there in your head, some cancer, gonna kill you?"

"No," said Jason. "No Cajun ever died of a heart attack. Too busy dying from bullet wounds and the clap." He laughed, but it was a small laugh.

"You ain't a Cajun," Bud said. "Your grandmama was a Cajun, but you ain't. You're just a hick."

"Damn," said Jason. "You got it bad, ain't you?"

"Yeah," Bud said. "I been thinking."

Jason looked hard at him. Bud looked tired, maybe a

little thinner than Fat Tuesday last year. "You got something wrong with you?" Jason asked. "You sick?"

"Mebbe," Bud said. "Not much. My stomach gone a little bad on me lately. But that ain't it," he said. "I just been thinking. It's gonna happen sometime. You, you're fat. Don't it worry you?"

"I got to get back outside," said Jason. "You want some more beer, you change your mind about them crawdads, let me know. I'll fix you up."

"Yeah," said Bud.

"Why don't you come on out," said Jason. "With the rest of us."

"Think I'll stay in here a while, Jase," Bud said. He turned back to the tv. A big woman, that looked like an opera singer, was on the screen now. Jason was glad the sound was off. He stayed for a minute, watching, then left.

As he walked out onto the porch, Jason saw that somebody had left a paper plate full of crawdad shells, mottled red and brown, sitting on a folding chair. He picked one up, looked at it, at the small black eyes and the legs, the segmented body.

"Does look kind of like a bug," he said.

*   *   *

There was a lot of noise and yelling going on outside. Jason looked for Sara, saw her standing next to Cousin Mobrey Davis' old Ford pick-em-up. He went to her.

"What's this?" he said.

Sara gestured to a knot of people standing nearby. "Mobrey," she said. Jason could hear Minnie Imogen's voice over the rest.

"You ain't taking that little girl anywhere," she was yelling, making a pretty good racket for a woman of her age. Jason saw Cousin Mobrey Davis, a smile on his face, trying to pat the old lady on the head.

"That's all right, granny," he said, "you jest don't worry." He stepped past Minnie Imogen, pushed through the knot of Sara's relatives who were standing around. Verna followed him, keeping her eyes on his broad back.

"Shameful," spat the old woman who Jason didn't know. He'd heard her name, couldn't recall it.

Jason stepped up to Cousin Mobrey. The other man stopped.

"Ho, Jase," Mobrey said.

"What's up, Mobrey," Jason said. The old women had ranged themselves a couple of yards away. "That girl's my responsibility," Minnie Imogen shouted. "You ain't going nowhere."

"You got them upset pretty good," Jason said.

Cousin Mobrey Davis swiveled his head to look at the women, blinked once, slowly. "Hell, you know them," he said. "I'm going acrost the causeway to N.O.," he said, "thought I'd take Verna here."

The girl ducked her head, smiled. She had dabbed at the stain on her blouse with a napkin, just made it worse.

"Do you know that she ain't never seen the Mardi Gras in the city?" said Cousin Mobrey Davis. "Girl ought to see that before she's too old. While she can 'preciate it."

Jason considered. "You want to go, do you, Verna?" he asked. "Go see the Mardi Gras?"

"Yessir," she said, very polite.

"See," said Mobrey Davis. "Ain't nothing wrong."

"Yuh," said Jason. "Well, you take care, Mobrey Davis." He stepped away from Mobrey, let him go past, get into the truck.

"You all have a good time," he said. He leaned in to Verna. "Get him to show you the sights, hear?" he said. He looked hard at Mobrey.

Mobrey cranked the old truck over, got it to start. "Yo," he said. "Thanks for the crawdads."

Then he went, blue smoke rolling out of the exhaust of the Ford. Jason watched him go. Through the back window of the truck, he could see Cousin Mobrey's big half-bald head, Verna's smaller golden one. He pressed both his hands on his stomach, sighed.

The two old women still stood not far off, with Sara's family behind them. "That damn Mobrey Davis," Minnie Imogen said. Jason turned on her.

"What'd you want me to do?" he said. "Was I supposed to stop them? Get you some food," he said. "Get you some food and be quiet."

"I'm leaving," said Minnie Imogen. "And so am I," said the other old woman.

"Just who the hell are you, anyway," Jason said, but he couldn't tell if she heard. She and Minnie Imogen were already on the way to the dusty Buick they'd come in.

"Goddam," Jason said, as the party broke up.

*   *   *

Bud Semples was the last to leave the Goodells' house. "See you," he said to Sara, and kissed her on the cheek. She smiled at him like she was tired, went into the house. Bud and Jason stood facing each other on the screen porch.

"Shoot," said Bud. "Family packed it in kind of early this year, didn't they?"

"Yuh," said Jason.

"Funny about Mobrey leaving with Verna, ain't it?"

"Don't mean nothing," Jason said. "He's just being nice."

"Nice yeah. Lot of people like to be nice that way," Bud said.

Jason squinted at him. "What do you want to say things

like that for?" Jason said.

"Like what?" Bud asked. "It's just the truth is all."

"Yuh," said Jason. "Well, mebbe folks don't want to hear everything you got to say, Bud. Mebbe sometimes folks could just do without it."

Bud looked surprised. "I guess that's so," he said.

"I guess it is," Jason said. They stood uncomfortably together for a minute.

"Well," said Bud. "I figure I'll get going." He paused a second. "Mebbe we'll get together, go into the city sometime?"

"Mebbe so," Jason said.

Bud left, his back tires throwing up gravel from the driveway as he went.

"Jesus Christ," Sara said from indoors.

"What is it, baby?" Jason called. He watched Bud's car roll down the road.

"Somebody's made just one hell of a mess in the tv room," she said. "Crawdads everwhere."

Jason could hear her moving the chairs around to get at the crawdads. One of them went over with a crash.

"You want to come in here, give me a hand?" Sara called. He stepped off the screen porch, walked past the empty burlap sack, the Hefty bag.

"Jason Goodell," Sara yelled. "You get your ass in here and help me."

Jason didn't answer. He touched his hand to the big black crawdad pot, and it was cold.

Water Witch

The locust pulls itself out of the ground and it is dry and sand-colored, like the grass and the ground and the scrub trees all around us. I watch it haul itself out of the hole, blind and dragging thin splintered wings behind it. I feel like I am watching something ancient creep up out of an Indian mound.

The boy is setting back on his haunches, peering at the locust. His hair is the color of sand too and it sticks up on the crown of his head. The denim shorts he is wearing are torn and sliding off his skinny hips. He don't have a shirt on and his skin is burned and flaking in places from the hot sun that is in the sky for fifteen hours a day.

I am tired and my head hurts like a bastard. I touch my forehead with the palm of my hand. The skin there is dry and cracked like a creek bed. The fever has sucked me dry.

The boy don't sweat either. He sets still, eyes on the locust which is struggling and dying now. The boy makes me think of a toad, squatting there in the dust watching it die. He pokes at the locust with a stick. It just lays there. You can just about see through its shell. It will never make it to the trees or even to a fence post to shed its skin and to lay its eggs.

I remember watching the locusts come out of the ground when I was a kid back home. The sun there was not near so hot as it is here and the ground was soft and cool. The locusts would come up by the dozens, hundreds, drill their little round holes through the dirt. They were wet-looking, looked like warm chocolate or dark jewels, rubbing their legs all over their bodies, stretching their wings to dry.

Me and my brother Sonny would grab them up to put and keep in jars. Smallmouth bass would hit a live locust like nothing else I ever seen. Been down there seven years, just waiting for us to need them to fish with, Sonny would say when he stuck a hook through one.

The boy sweeps the locust away with his stick, hitches the shorts higher up, squints his eyes at me. They are green eyes and make me think of still water. A speckled trout would sleep in water like that, if there was rocks to hide in.

'Nother dry one I say. There is skin peeling from the boy's collarbone. He scratches at it, looks away from me. Dry is all he knows these last three years and I am the one that has caused it.

I put my hand on the boy's narrow shoulder and he lets it lay there, don't even bother to shrug it off. His skin is cooler than mine. He ain't got a fever from all the sun and heat. A kid can live with most anything. Son I say but I can't think of anything more.

With his bare foot he steps on the locust, puts the hard callus of his heel down on it. I hear its shell pop when it crushes, take my hand off the boy. Real slow he scrapes his foot on the rock-hard ground, pivots on his heel like putting out a butt. It feels like something has gone soft and rotten inside me, looking at him. I can count each rib where the thin skin covers it, could trace over the back-bones with my middle finger where they curve up to his shoulders.

I am a big man, better than six feet and two hundred pounds, and it scares me to think about how small the boy is, how small his mother is. I am afraid that, touching them sometime, I may punch through the thin skin and the balsa-wood ribs and bones, into the guts that twitch and jump inside. I am afraid that the dry has made them brittle, made it so I might hurt them or kill them just by touching. The boy walks away from me through the short stiff grass.

The water table will rise I call out to him. He knows it for a lie.

The stock is just about dead from the heat and there is no way to get them anything like enough water. They are ruined anyhow from being dry so long, and I probably should of killed them some time ago. Their tongues are thick and roped with dried slobber and they stand stiff-legged with their mouths open, blowing like furnaces when I feed them. I got to give them feed because the grass is no good. The heat that comes off of them when you stand near is like a sickness.

The heat rising off the ground makes the boy appear to flicker like the flame of a kerosene lamp. I close my eyes against the pain in my head. Christ I think, it is all gone to hell. I slam my fists against my belly again and again.

Where we come from, the mountains kept the sun off for most of the day but for half a dozen hours and the sleeping was sweet. Here there are no mountains but the land just rolls and rolls and there is nothing to keep the sun off.

I scratch at my stomach and it is hard and scaled, the belly of a lizard or armadillo. The peeling skin packs up under my fingernails. I wonder what is under the skin, if I could scratch and pull it all away. I wonder if I am becoming an animal underneath, some kind of thing that lives in the dirt and the sun without any water.

The boy is in amongst the scrub trees now where I can't see. I walk after him. My boots click on the ground. Come out from there and let's go back to the house I shout. There are lizards in the trees and the shells of a few locusts that made it through the dry.

One lizard, a gecko, looks at me from where it is splayed out on the trunk of a little twisted scrub tree. It is yellow and blends in good with the trunk of the tree. If I look at it for a time I can lose it against the bark, just make it go away. Then I see it again, its breathing. That is the only movement it makes. Its sides pump in and out.

I got to go into town I shout to the boy. I can't see him at all now.

You can come if you want I say.

He is gone and it is just me there in the scrub. When I look, the lizard has gone from where he was setting. I have to shade my eyes and look a couple of times to be sure.

I got no time for this I say. I know the shooting will take most of the day and I ain't got shells enough in the house for it. I got to go in town and get some. I want it to be done. I turn and head out of the scrub, back toward the house.

*   *   *

Hod hands me a Tecate, squints up at the sky like he is looking for a cloud. Hod is a great fat man that owns a grain and hardware store in Brenham. The beer is warm but even so the bottle is sweating. I take a swallow of my beer and Hod takes a gulp of his. He nods at me.

Got to drink these all day just to keep alive he says.

I say Liquor don't help. Ever time you take a drink of liquor, it takes a drink of you too. Dries you out real bad.

Hod shakes his head like I don't know what I'm talking about. That's just hard liquor he says. Beer cools you down.

He finishes off the bottle and drops it down beside him, snags another out of the cooler he's got next his chair. The ice has long ago melted and the bottles is just setting in water. He snaps the top off the Tecate, wraps his lips around the mouth of the bottle. Nothing moves in his mouth or throat that I can see. He just pours the beer down. There is dirt in the wrinkles of his face.

We stay there like that for a couple minutes, out on the porch of Hod's store, him setting in an old half-busted ladder-back chair, me leaning in the doorway, sucking on the bottle. Then Hod turns to me and a button on his work shirt comes undone. I can see a piece of his big hairy gut, pale and loose from drinking and setting all day long. There's big dark stains under the arms of his shirt and down his back where he's sweated out all that beer that he has took in. Hod smells like a barley field.

I hear your well give in Hod says.

We got some collapse I say. When the water table dropped.

You still got water? he says. He ain't looking at me anymore, just out at the empty street. I don't remember a car going by while I been there. I would bet this ain't the first time he has had this same conversation.

It still pumps a little I say. Not near enough.

We are quiet again. A car finally goes past and the breeze it brings with it is hot and dirty, smells like scorched motor oil.

I want to buy some shells is why I come by I say.

Time for some cattle to die Hod says. I don't say anything back.

Castle, you about the last one he says.

I figure Hod must wish he was dead when he gets up in the morning and all that fat and beer pulls him down toward the ground. For just a minute I feel good because I am much younger and stronger than this old man here in front of me.

Most the other stock around here been dead for weeks he says. He gestures at the sky. The devil been keeping the knacker some busy this season he says.

I put the bottle down.

I got a lot of feed I ain't gonna be using this season I say.

He crosses his short arms. Wish I could help you, hoss, but I'm way overstocked myself he says. Ain't much of a market for feed in Brenham.

No I say, I guess not. Just figured I would ask.

I go inside the store and it is stifling in there, like the building saves up the heat of the day. I understand why Hod sits out on the porch. The fever is on me again and I clench my teeth to keep from shivering. Crazy to shiver in a place as hot as this.

You go on in and find what you're needing Hod says from out on the porch. Shells are in behind the front counter.

I go around behind the register, scout through the cartridge boxes for 30–30 hollow points. A box of fifty I figure will do me. They are nearly nine dollars the box, so I leave a ten on the counter. It is not worth rousing Hod up to get me my change. The box of shells will not fit in my pocket so I carry it out to the truck in my hand.

It's a goddam shame Hod says as I'm getting in the truck. You got a nice place out there, nice little kid. How's Min he asks.

Min is tired and hot and she is full of hate I could say, but I don't. OK I say and pull the door to. I crank the engine over and the truck starts right away. I can hear the valve lifters ticking away in there, going bad, but there is not much to do about that.

See you around Hod shouts to me from where he sets on his porch, waving the brown bottle of beer at me as I go.

* * *

The heat demons coming up off the road make everthing seem as if it might be a dream. The truck sways and shudders on the nine-foot right of way like it is a high wind out there but the air is dead still and heavy, like it is water I'm driving through.

Some longhorn beef off to one side of the gravel road stand like they are dead, struck by lightning and still on their feet. They are gray with dust from the road. In a couple minutes, the dust that I have raised will drift down and settle on them too.

I got the box of shells on the passenger seat of the truck and it jiggles and clinks as I drive. I blink the sweat out of my eyes and see there is somebody standing on the gravel berm of the road, got his thumb in the air.

I don't really want company but I am pulling over before I know it and the drifter gets in the truck cab with me. He is tall and strong, some years younger than me, smells like a hot day of walking down an empty road. He wears an Aggies tee shirt cut off at the rib cage that shows his hard flat stomach muscles. He pushes the shells over on the bench seat, stretches out. His hair is blond and too long.

Hot one out there for walking he says. The heels on his boots are worn down and the boot leathers are walked over to one side.

Speak of the weather to me and I'll have to kill you I say.

He laughs and his teeth are white and square in his mouth, large teeth like the people on tv.

Must be a cattle rancher he says. He looks around the cab of the pickup, fingers the 30–30 I got in the rack behind my head, glances at the box of shells.

Guess I know what them shells is for he says. Everbody is shooting their cattle from the dry. I guess they must be about a hundred miles of ditches dug for cattle just in this end of the state alone he says.

The drifter smiles like he thinks that is no doubt a good thing. The end-loaders been running pretty steady lately, digging and filling, digging and filling. It takes a big hole to cover a single steer, a deep hole, and it is a lot more than just one steer that has died. It don't pay anything to take them to slaughter.

I got a little place, few dozen white face I say. I was doing ok I say, but my well give in. Just a trickle of water now and I can't see any good letting them dry up. I just don't see the good in that I say.

The drifter leans back and puts his right arm out the window of the truck, waves it in the hot wind that rushes past. Behind us, dust rises fifty feet in the air from the road, a gray trail lifting back a quarter mile, blinding anybody that's on the road behind us. I know if Min or the boy is looking out the door of the place, they'll see the dust coming down the road and know it is me.

Now ain't you lucky to of picked me up the drifter says. He laughs and it is a high, unsteady laugh, more like the whicker of a goat than a laugh.

How's that I say. I can't see it at all.

'Cause when you're out of water he says, you went and picked up the best water witch in East Texas.

I look at him leaning against the door of the truck. You

got to be kidding I say. It has been a long time since I have heard of a water witch.

No joke he says and his face gets real serious. It makes him look older when he frowns. You feed me he says and I will find you water. I found water in the desert before he says.

You got to do a miracle to find water out here I say. There ain't any.

I done miracles he says. His voice is very low and calm.

You bet I say. What the hell. I got no better answers and I am not looking forward to shooting the cattle.

I turn off the nine-foot road and onto my place. The gravel spins up under the wheels of the truck and kicks against the rocker panels. The drifter ain't looking at me. He's looking at the house, out in the middle of a field of dead yellow grass.

* * *

Min looks the drifter up and down and there is no appreciation in her for his good looks. She tilts her head to one side and stares at him with narrow eyes but it don't make him nervous at all. Who might this be, Castle she says to me like he ain't even in the room at all.

Her hair is pulled back tight against her temples and her feet are bare and gray with dust. She suffers the dry worse than anybody. I learned how you take a dry shower my time in the Navy and the boy don't care if he don't get clean for a week.

Min don't understand why the cattle ain't dead yet, why they are still drinking our water. I toss the box of shells on the kitchen table and she looks at it, back at the drifter. She has made *fajitas* for supper, and I figure that is good because it is always easy to stretch the Mex food.

There is water near this place and I aim to find it for you the drifter says. He spreads his arms wide and it is like a preacher saying it. I figure Min will laugh at him and tell him to get out of her place, give me hell for bringing some scruffy kid home to feed. It don't happen that way though. She is looking at him and I can tell she is interested in what he's saying.

Water he says and it is like a magic word, like I can feel it trickling down my limbs and along my back. The boy comes in from the back room and stares at the drifter too. Water the witch says and puts his head back, closes his eyes. Tears squeeze out from under his eyelids, run down his cheeks, streak the dirt that is laying there. His voice is deep and rolls through the room like the sound of a bell.

It is a fire and a magnet he says, a great electric current that runs through the rotted limestone earth. I can lead you to it he says. He holds his hands up. My hands show it he says. It is in my hands. When I was born all the geese in my momma's flock died. I was born with a caul over my face, a flap of skin as white and as thin as a bedsheet. When my daddy saw me, he looked at the fingers of my hand and he knew that I was something special.

I see that the middle finger and the pointer finger on both his hands are the same length. I don't know when I seen hands like that before, but whether it is a sign of anything I don't know. Min is looking at his hands too. He waves them in the air, slams them down on the table top.

It is a gift from God he says, this thing that I can do. He is shouting now and I am scared listening to him.

A gift from God, to bring aid to man he says. He moves to Min and takes her chin in his hand. He has to look down to see into her face. A tear hangs off the end of his nose, drops onto Min's cheek. She blinks at him, looks like she is trying to wake from a dream. The boy is next to her, hanging off her skirt.

Water to wash he shouts into her face. His voice is like a hammer. He seems awful strong and I hear a roaring in my ears that is not just his voice.

Water to drink he says, to splash and play in. He pushes her back against the cabinets, still his hand on her chin. I take a step toward him.

Gushing water, water that don't stop, water that runs and cools and cuts the dirt he says. Min's head moves, up and down, and I can't see if it is her moving or him tugging her chin. Water he says and touches her hair. Water he says and he touches the flesh of her face. Water and he takes the collar of her dress between his fingers.

Water she says and her voice is small and tired, almost swallowed up by his shouting.

I put a hand on the drifter's shoulder and he spins on me real fast. I almost expect a knife, hold up my hands in front of me but he just looks at me with these electric blue eyes. Water for the pump he says. Water for the stock.

You can get it I say, but it is a question. I wonder what I would of done if it had been a knife in his hand. Something about him, the set of his square shoulders or the way he holds his head, says that it might of been, might just as well of been, and you better watch out.

It is there he says, and I can get it.

All right I say, but no more of this. This is craziness. I gesture at Min. She is watching us and the boy is still behind her.

What, the witch says. All that about the hands and the caul? That's the truth he says. God's honest truth, mister.

The fire is gone out of his eyes. It is like someone large has left the room and taken a lot of the air with him. I look the drifter up and down, wonder if he can really find water. There is nothing about him now that makes me think he could find water under the dry blowing dirt of this farm.

* * *

The boy wakes in the night and he is crying. I lay there for a time listening to him, breathe in with a sob, breathe out long and loud. He has stopped needing to cry now but is keeping on with it, figuring one of us will hear him and come in to help him get back to sleep. Min is breathing deep, still asleep over on her side of the bed.

I rise up and walk into the boy's room. The drifter is still asleep on the couch where we put him down for the night. There wasn't enough day left for him to do his witching, so we fed him supper and put him up, figure he will do his job or not early in the morning.

With just a couple of hours to go till dawn it is hard to believe that before long we may have water. I wonder if I am being a fool listening to this skinny kid, what he says about finding water for us on this dry farm, but there is not much else to do. Besides, it has kept me from having to shoot the cattle for another day.

The boy is looking at me. You should be asleep I say to him. It's late.

I was dreaming he says. I was dreaming about being home.

When he says home I know he don't mean Texas. This never has been home for him.

It was wet and green he says. There are tears in his eyes and I marvel he has got enough in him to let him cry. He is a tough little boy for his age. I am glad he will talk to me now, in the middle of the night.

I know it was I say.

He is laying on top of his covers, just got his underpants on because of the heat. I can hardly believe how skinny his legs look. That is how some kids are I know, but this seems like a sickness to me. When he looks at me it is like the cattle with their hollow eyes and the way the hot breath rasps in their throats.

I seen a little stream that come out of the rocks and run real fast downhill he says. I was drinking out of it.

That was right near the house I say. A place just like that and I guess you just remember it.

I guess he says. He closes his eyes.

Can you sleep okay now I ask. He nods his head on the pillow. I kiss him on the forehead, feel how hot and dry he is. When I leave the room, he is already breathing deep and even, and I envy him his dreams. He is the only one of us that can get back, seems like.

On the way back to bed I stand by the couch, watch the water witch in his sleep. His lips move just a little bit, and they are ragged where he has chewed them. He is a strong man I can see but there is nothing magic about him. He has his arms wrapped around himself.

You best be able to do it I say to him while he sleeps. You best not to come into my home and eat my food and give me hope unless you are able to pull it off I say. I wonder if it is water that he dreams about.

I will kill you if you have given me false hope I say to him. That is the bargain I make with myself, standing next to the couch in the middle of the night. That is the bargain I make, and I know I will keep by it, even when the hot sun is in the sky.

* * *

Have you ever seen water witching done the boy in the Aggies tee shirt asks me. He wants to get an early start on the day so we are up before the rest of the house.

I seen it when I was a kid I say. My daddy wanted a new well for the house so he hired this guy that we knew. He was a tall old guy that always wore a long gray coat, even when it was hot. He was the spirit of water, he used to say. He didn't say he could find water, he said he was it and it was him.

That's how it feels the kid says to me.

He used a bent ash twig I say. I hope you ain't going to need an ash twig.

No ash twig the kid says. If you got the power you can use most anything. I use coat hangers mostly.

It was not hard to find water back there I say to him. It was limestone rock and most anywhere you drilled there was water. It will not be that easy here.

It don't have to be easy the kid says and I am impressed with how confident he is. We may have to dig deep but the water will be there.

If he is a con man, he is a good one. Maybe he is just crazy. Maybe he can do it.

Two metal coat hangers is what I need he says.

When I get them he works the wire until it breaks from fatigue. He bends the wire until he has got two right angles, holds them loose in his hands, walks around in the near field.

When they cross there is water he says. The harder they swing, the more water and the closer to the surface. Since you got no drilling equipment, we got to find it close to the top he says.

They ain't none close to the top I say. I am not going to believe in him until he proves it to me.

Don't tell me he says. He walks away from me, still

holding the bent coat hangers loose in his hands. As I watch, they swing toward one another and then away. I can't tell if he is moving them or not.

When he is more than a hundred yards from me, he calls out.

Here it is he says. A river of water and near to the surface. This is the place we dig.

It has only taken him about twenty minutes to find the place. I wonder how it could be so quick when everthing is as dry as it is.

They swung hard did they I ask him.

He holds out his hands to me, drops the coat hangers to the ground. Burned my palms it swung so hard he says. I can see his palms are red like he says, but what it means I am afraid to say.

* * *

By the time we get to eight feet, I know we are not going to strike water. We have to broaden out the hole so we don't hit each other with our shovel blades, have to shore up the walls with planks. Pretty soon we have to take turns in the hole because we can't make it big enough for both of us.

In the hole it is hot and damp from the dirt crumbling on all sides. The damp don't mean nothing. It is just that the dry hasn't turned the whole world to dust yet. Dirt is always damp this far down. My first turn down there I have to climb out after only about fifteen minutes of throwing dirt. It seems to me like all the air in the hole has been breathed before, like I will drop if I stay in there too long.

I can still feel it he calls out to me from up top. He is conning me I now know. There is no water down here. Where you would expect to find hundreds of worms and beetles there is just a few dozen. He expects to keep me digging for a couple days and maybe take off with the truck or something when we are asleep.

Maybe he just wants something to eat, a place to bed down a while, and he figures this is a good way to get it. I bet it has worked for him before, in a land where we need water so bad. A man that makes people think there is water in the dry don't deserve to walk the earth.

The boy comes out to where we are digging while I am in the hole. Looking up, I see his face next to the water witch's, leaning over.

You finding any water the boy says to me. He looks like he don't care much one way or the other. I figure he has forgotten about his dream from last night.

Go on back to the house I say.

He keeps on looking down at me, don't move. He looks at me like he wonders what I am doing down in all that dirt, down in the hole.

Better mind your daddy the water witch says to him. We got some work to do he says.

The boy moves back away where I can't see him and it is just the witch's face against the bright light overhead. It is good that the boy will be in the house. I don't want him to see what is coming.

He's a good boy the witch says to me.

Yes he is I say.

It is awful easy to make good on my promise. It is so easy it makes me know I am right to do it, even though I ain't a murderer.

When I come out after my third time in the hole, I am covered in dirt. I lean over to catch my breath and the water witch starts his way down into the hole. It is well into the afternoon now and as hot as it is going to get in the day. The little herd of white face I got drifts past us not too far away and I know I will have to do them too.

My turn he says as he goes down into the hole. I give it to him right on the top of the head with the edge of my shovel and he drops down into the hole, which is much deeper than a grave now. He falls down in without a scream or a cry and just lays there in the bottom. He might be trying to fool me again, but I don't think so.

Yo, water witch I call down into the hole. Still he don't say anything back to me. I see where the cut on the top of his head is oozing a little. I figure a shovel swung like that could bite into a man pretty deep.

He don't make any noise when I put back the first shovelful of dirt on top of him, or the second or the third. When fifteen shovels have gone into the hole, I know I have killed him and I cover him up as fast as I can. It is faster to fill a hole than it is to dig it, and I am done by about supper time.

I got a little pile of dirt that I don't have to use to fill the hole. There is always a little dirt left over when you dig a hole and fill it again, but I figure most of this is what the water witch has displaced. From the dirt that I don't have to use, he is not as big a man as I had thought. He couldn't have weighed over a hundred and fifty pounds.

* * *

Where did the water witch go to Min asks me as I come into the house. I stamp some dust off my boots, look up at her. It is easy to lie to her. She would not understand what a man has to do sometimes. I couldn't expect her to understand.

He run off I say. There wasn't any water out there and he knew it. When he saw he wasn't getting anything off us, he just lit out up the road. Hitchhiking, like before.

I empty the box of 30–30 cartridges into my pocket where it will be easy to get at them. Min watches me.

You going to kill the cattle she says. Though she has waited for this a long time, she sounds upset about it now. She is glad it is my job and not hers.

Got to do it sometime I say. I put it off way too long as it is.

And what then she says to me.

Then we take the boy and we go home I say.

Home she says like she can't believe it. But we got nothing there. We sold it all to come down here.

After this we got nothing here I say, and I pat my pockets. Then I head out into the evening.

The sun is going down, and for the first time in a long while, the breeze is cool. I pass the mound of dirt where the water witch lies, further down than most men get buried.

I leave boot tracks in the soft dirt, crouch down for just a second, but I don't feel anything special there. No water, no ghosts. It is just a spot in the ground, like the farm, like the ditch they will dig with an end-loader for all the cattle. It is nothing I can't leave behind me.

Town Smokes

My daddy been in the ground a couple hours when it starts to rain. Hunter's up on the porch, strippen away at a chunk of soft pine wood with his Kaybar knife, and I'm setten out in the yard to get away from the sound, chip chip chip like some damn squirrel. Hunter moves in his seat as he whittles, can' sit still.

It's big drops that are comen down, and starten real quick, like you wouldn' of expected it at all. I look up when it comes on to rain, and what I see of sky's just as blue and clear. Happen like that up here sometimes, my daddy's told me, that you get your hard rain and your blue sky, and both together like that. First time I seen it though, that I recall.

You gonna drown out there Hunter says to me, and I can just hardly hear him over the rain pounden into the dirt of the yard and spangen off the tin roof.

What's that I say. He's not more'n ten yard from me but there's rain like a sheet between us, getten in my eyes and my ears and down my collar. I like the way the cool rain feels as it soaks my shirt. I catch a couple drops in my mouth, and they got no taste to them at all. The rain washes the sweat and the dirt off me.

Drown like a turkey in the rain Hunter says. Out there and mouth open. He gets up to go inside, drops the wood and the knife down into the chair. The heavy knife sticks in the seat, blade down. Hunter moves like an old man, older than my daddy, fat and tired. He ran the sweat like a hog when we was diggen before, because the dirt was hard and packed where we put the grave, out behind the house. I thought his heart might vapor-lock on him there for a while, all red and breathen through the mouth as he was.

Hunter slips the straps of his overalls as he goes inside and I know he will spend the rest of the day in his under-wear sluggen bourbon and listenen to the radio.

Get in out the rain he says to me back over his shoulder. I stay out in the yard until the door swings shut behind him. The ground is getten soft under my sneakers but I know that is just the top dirt. It hasn' rained for a good long while and the clay dirt has got dry. The rain comes down too fast and hard to soak in. I know it will not get down deep at all.

I go to the door and I can smell the piece of wood Hunter's been cutten on, the sharp pine sap. It's a tooth he's carven out, like a big boar's tusk, all smooth and curved comen out of the rough wood. He carves a lot of things like that.

He's my daddy's brother that lives with us at the camp up on Tree Mountain. He's a big man, has this small head that sits on his body like a busted chimney on a house. He don' talk much. Old Hunter'll surprise you, how good he is with whittlen. He's sold some things in town.

Water rollen off the roof runs deep around the edges of the porch. Out of the rain, my wet clothes are heavy on me. Against my leg, cold in my pocket, I feel the arrowhead I found in my daddy's grave. Flint hunten point with the edges still sharp. It wasn' very far down, only mebbe five inches. I didn' know this's a good place to find arrowheads. I'll dig again later in other spots to look for some more. I lick my lips, want a smoke, a Camel mebbe.

You got a cigarette I say, goen into the house.

Get your fucken shoes off, bringen wet in the house Hunter says. He's standen in the front room in his shorts, and his hair stands up like he's been runnen his hands through it. The radio he keeps back in his room is on to a news station. What's a fourteen-year-old boy want with a cigarette anyway he says.

Fifteen I say. My shoes come off my feet with a wet noise. I got no socks on, and the wood floor is rough. I know to be careful in bare feet or get a sliver.

I ain' got a cigarette he says.

You got a pinch then I say. I know he's got no snuff but I ask anyway.

Hunter sits down. He's got the bottle in his hand. Christ Jesus he says. You visit whores too?

These are things a man does I say. I guess I just feel like a smoke.

I laugh but Hunter don' join in. He looks at me. When I keep my eyes on him he looks away, out the window. The hard rain throws up a spray of mist and you can' see for more than a couple yards. The roof of the camp is fairly new and tight and it don' leak at all. Hunter and my daddy put it on just the last summer before this one and they did a good job. I carried tacks and tin sheets for them, always scared of slippen and fallen off the roof.

Real gulley-washer Hunter says. They got to watch for them flash floods down to the valley. Farms goen to lose a lot of dirt to the river, this don' let up.

He keeps on looken out the window and all the time the rain is getten harder. It's finally dark out there, clouds coveren the sun. We are high up and it is strange to see it dark in the middle of day. Generally we get hard bright mountain light that makes you squint to look at it.

Your daddy used to make his own smokes Hunter says.

I say I know.

Mebbe you look through his traps, you find you the fixens he says.

That's a thought I say. I don' make any move to the room my daddy and I share, did share. I stand and drip on the floor and listen to the rain. Hunter looks at me like watchen a snake or mebbe a dog that you ain' sure of. The rain outside the windows makes it look like it ain' any place in the world but the camp and us in it. We're alone here. I think mebbe the rain won' let up for a while yet.

Hunter says You do what you want. Always done it that way anyhow didn' you.

He stands, works his shoulders back and forth. He is sore from the diggen and would like his muscles rubbed I know. Rain throbs him some these days.

I'm gonna listen to the radio for a time he says.

I make a bet with myself he will be asleep before long.

The door to Hunter's room don' shut just right, so when he closes it I can still get the sound from the radio in his room. It is a station from in the valley. The announcer says to watch for flash floods in the narrow, high-banked creeks comen down off the mountain. He says it like it is the mountain's fault.

The tower of the radio is on top of a ridge not far from the camp. The place where they put it is a couple hunnerd feet higher than where we are and you can see it from the porch of the camp on a good day. They took out a whole big stand of blue spruce to get it in.

From where we are, the clearen looks smooth and clean and well took care of, like a yard, but I have been up there a couple time—it ain' such a hard climb as it looks, just a couple hours scramble—and it is a mess around the base of that tower. Vines and creepers around the base and grass to your knees. The blue spruce are comen back too and they are fast-growen trees.

Hunter snaps off the radio and I hear him stretch out on to his bed. He keeps moven around like he will never get to sleep.

* * *

My daddy's things is all over the room in no particular order. It is like he is still there, in all them traps, though I know that he is cold and dead and under the earth not a dozen yards away.

These things are mine now I say but it is not like they belong to me at all. Some of them should go to Hunter. I ain' sure that I want that Hunter should have them, though I would be hard put to say why not.

I move the rifle that is layen on my daddy's bed, the heavy lever-action Marlin, and the cartridge belt that is layen there too. My fingers touch the cool blued metal of the barrel and I know I will have to clean the metal where I touched it, rub it down with a patch of oiled cloth. There is nothen that is worse for any good piece of metal than the touch of a man's hand my daddy would always be sayen.

It is two guns that are in my family, both my daddy's, his old Marlin and the single-action Colt .38 that his grandaddy used sometime way back in the Philippine Insurrection. I put the Colt down on the bed next the rifle, fish out a box of rounds for it as well. From the feel, there ain' too many cartridges left to the box, which is tore up and very old. Beside the guns and his clothes, there is not much else of his in the room.

In the top of the old chifferobe I find his little sack for tobacco. There is not much that is left in the sack, and I can bet that it is pretty old and dry. He was not much for a smoker and a sack of tobacco had a long life around him. There is a paper book of matches next the tobacco with all but two of the matches gone. It is from the Pioneer, which is a bar I have seen down to the valley. There is also a couple bills, a five and a one. I pocket the money.

I scratch through the rest of his stuff in the drawer—a dog whistle and a couple loose .410 rounds for a gun that we ain' even got; needles and thread in a sewen kit; some Vietnamese money that he used to keep around for a laugh—and come up with his old Barlow clasp knife and his Gideon's. The clasp knife I toss down with the rest of the pieces that I figure I might take with me. It clicks off the barrel of the Colt and leaves a mark on the metal. That is one mark that I won' get a hiden for.

The Gideon's is old and slippery in my hand and missen many pages. My daddy has used it for a lot of years. The paper is thin and fine for rollen your own; if you are good you can get two smokes to the page. As I say, he was not a heavy smoker and he is not even gotten up to the New Testament yet, just somewhere in Jeremiah.

I pull out the next page and crease it with my middle finger, tap tobacco onto the paper. The tobacco is crumbly with age and breaks into small pieces; it is very dark brown and cheap-looken. Some of it sticks to my skin. I lay down on the bed and put the home-rolled cigarette in my mouth. Pieces of tobacco stick to my tongue. I spit out, light the smoke.

Christ I say. The cigarette don' taste good at all, like the tobacco has rotted. I flick it out onto the floor and sparks fly off from the lit end. They stick to the wood floor and smolder there, and one by one the sparks burn themselves out.

*   *   *

I figure I will go into town for a time I say to Hunter's back.

He is face down on the narrow cot in his room and I figure him for asleep. The bottle is by the bed and it is several fingers down from where it was earlier. Hunter's back is pale and wide, and there is a mole I never took notice of before in the deep track that his backbone makes.

He says Goen where? and rolls over so sudden it startles me. His face is wet with tears and it surprises me that this old man has been cryen. For a minute I can' remember why. The bed sags under him.

Down the mountain I say. Get me some smokes mebbe.

He is wipen at his face with his arm, drunk and embarrassed that I seen him cry. You can cry for your brother I want to say.

You ain' comen back are you Hunter says.

He puts a foot on the floor and the bottle goes over. I pick it up for him, set it back where it was. It is all but empty with haven been dumped out. The floor is damp and the room smells of bourbon. I look out the little window in Hunter's bedroom and the rain has slacked off some. That is a help.

The rifle's in on the bed I say. He would of wanted for you to have it.

I walk out into the front room and Hunter comes after me, walken in his underwear and bare feet. I got the .38 and the clasp knife and all in my kit with me, ready to go.

Why is it that you're goen now Hunter says. With the rain and all. It's a bad day to be goen down to the valley.

I think about that. It is not somethen I have thought about much before this. I look at him.

Because I am tired I say. Tired of the mountain and smoken shitty tobacco. Mebbe I just want to smoke a real cigarette for a change.

Want you some town smokes I guess Hunter says.

I say I guess.

Mebbe want to kiss all them pretty girls down to the valley too Hunter says. I don' say anythen.

Yeah he says. Bring me back a bottle when you come.

I'll do that I say. You bet.

I go outside and the air is cool for a day in the middle of summer. The rain has turned the dust to mud, and water runs in streams in the yard, has bit into the dirt. A hard rain for just a couple hours I know can raise the creeks and cut right through the banks and dirt levees down below. I wonder what they are doen with all the water down in the town. The air feels damp but the rain is mostly stopped.

Hunter has followed me out into the yard and his feet are all over mud. How you goen down? he says.

Railroad right of way I say. It's the quickest way.

Hunter follows me the next couple of steps and I cut from the yard into the underbrush so he will stop followen. The leaves on the bushes are wet and soak my shirt, my kit. I know the damp will be hard on the gun.

Ought not to of happened to your daddy that way Hunter says. He is looken in the bushes like he can' see where I am at, but he wants me to hear him.

When the tree falls I say best the man that cut it should be out the way.

That is hard Hunter says to the bushes. That a boy should say that about his daddy that brought him up and fed him.

I know that Hunter will see me if I keep on talken. I don' want that he should see me. I turn and go, headen toward the right of way down the mountain.

We should of had someone to say the words Hunter calls after me. It ain' right that there wasn' nobody to say the words for him.

I keep goen through the brush. I guess I would of said the words if I knew them. I ain' got the least idee what words he would of wanted though.

*　*　*

The last time I seen my daddy he tells me a story. He has the old two-stroke loggen saw over his shoulder and is headed out to where he known there's some trees that has come down, or are ready to come down anyhow. You want some help daddy I ask and he says no.

Then he looks over at where Hunter is sitten on the porch and this time Hunter is carven a great horned owl out of a big piece of oak that would have gone well in the fire in the winter.

Hunter wasn' always so fat and lazy he says loud enough that he knows Hunter can hear him. Hunter don' stir from his carven, usen a chisel instead of the Kaybar knife. That's how he works on the ones he figures to sell.

Nawsir my daddy says, was a time when he and I used to run and raise some hell in these parts. When we was about your age. I 'member one time down to Seldomridge's place, little shorthorn farm next the river. You recall that Hunter?

Hunter keeps quiet, just gouges a long chunk of wood out the owl's back. It kind of ruins how the owl looks I think.

The river was froze over, couple three feet thick out near the banks my daddy says. Ice got all thin and black out toward the middle though where the water's deep and fast.

He shifts the chain saw from one shoulder to the other and I see where a little gas mixed with oil has leaked onto his shirt. He don' seem to mind.

So Hunter here riles up Seldomridge's cattle and about a dozen shorthorns go plowen out onto the ice my daddy says.

My daddy's starten to laugh and there are these tears formen in the corners of his eyes. I can hardly stand to look at him because he thinks the story is so funny and I don' get it at all yet.

And they're shiveren out there my daddy keeps on. Can hardly stand, all spraddle-legged and tryen to stay up on the ice, blowen and snorten, scared and full of snot and droolen, them whiteface. Hunter's yellen and holleren at them from the bank, just to keep them on the move, keep them up and off from the shore. Hunter's voice sounds loud out there with everthen else so quiet and covered in snow.

Then the first one goes through my daddy says and he can hardly keep the saw on his shoulders for laughen.

It sounds like a pistol shot when the ice gives and the steer disappears down and it's just black black water shooten up through the hole in the ice like a geyser. That sets them off, stompen and bellowen and the next goes through the ice, skitteren and scrabblen, and the next after that one. Prob'ly half a dozen, one after the other, they get out on the thin ice in the middle and don' have time to look surprised 'fore they go down.

And you was laughen Hunter says from behind his carven.

You damn right I was too my daddy says. I was laughen like a son of a bitch he says and he wheels and heads off into the woods after the tree that fell on him. As he goes, me and Hunter can hear him in the woods there, laughen and laughen about the whiteface that went through the ice in the middle of the river.

Them cattle showed up as far down the river as Teaberry Hunter says after my daddy is gone.

Drownded I ask.

Dead as hammers he says. You bet.

*   *   *

About halfway down the mountain a pig runs across the right of way just a couple feet in front of me. Scares the bejesus out of me, cutten out of the brush on one side and nearly steps on me goen past. It gets stuck for a second goen across the rails and I see that it is young, just a little spotted sucklen and haven a hard time of it. It is whinen a little as it gets over the belly-high steel rails, tail twitchen like a dog's. When it gets over the far rail it turns toward me a second and its eyes are rolled way back in its head. Then it gets into the brush on the other side of the right of way and it's gone.

Two boys come out of the brush after it and they are right on top of me too. Christ one of them says and shoves at me. He is not very big and I knock him down with my kit. The other is big and red-haired and carryen a rifle. He rushes across the right of way and stares into the brush. Goddam it to hell he says.

He raises the rifle, pointen into the brush after the sucklen, and I think for a minute that he is goen to let go.

Then I realize the pig must be in under cover now and he'd be a fool to shoot. Still his finger curves on the trigger a second, tugs and almost fires.

It is a short-barrelled Winchester carbine that he is carryen with a shrouded front sight for brush-beaten. The stock is wrapped around with black electric tape and there is rust all on the receiver. They are rough-looken boys. The big one is about my age and the little one some younger I figure.

The big red-headed one turns around to me and his eyes are cold. I figure he is mad because they lost the pig that they had been tracken. He drops the hammer back into half-cock, holds the rifle easy in the crook of his arm. His clothes are dirty and too small on his big frame.

Le's get a move on Okie the little one says. His teeth are gone rotten on him and make him talk odd, real soft like his mouth pains him. He says mebbe we can still get us that 'ere pig.

You hush Darius the big one says and he is still looken at me. It makes me nervous and I turn to head on down the cinder roadbed. The cinders are soft with the rain. They stick to the bottoms of my shoes, make my feet feel heavy. It is hard to walk on the railroad ties though, because they are too close together to make for an easy stride.

When I look back the big one, Okie, is still staren at me from under the long red hair. He licks his lips.

Hold up there a minute he says.

The little one trots after me a couple steps and I see there is somethen wrong with his legs, how they are too short for the rest of his body is what makes him so small. He is mebbe not so young as I first thought, mebbe older than me or Okie too. The ties are just right for him and he moves from one to the next without any trouble at all. Okie stays where he is.

We lost that 'ere shoat Darius says and he sounds like on the edge of cryen about it. You seen it he says.

Darius is right up on me now where I can smell him and I stop.

You boys want to let me alone I say. I ain' botheren you none.

Who says you was Okie calls out.

He's got the rifle pointen up at the gray sky now, held in both hands. He spits on the cinders, got a pinch of snuff in the right side of his mouth. He comes down the track a way, smilen, and I see his teeth are gone bad on him too. The snuff'll do that to you in time.

What you got Darius is sayen and I catch him looken at my kit. He's got his hands out like a kid asken for a candy. I drop the bag, push it back behind me. Darius is hoppen back and forth from one railroad tie to the other. He's got mud to the knee on his old corduroy pants, but it seems like he don' want to touch foot down on the roadbed.

He don' want you messen with his stuff Okie says to Darius. It is like a man talken to a kid.

He looks at me. You headen down into town he says. You live up on the mountain? He points back up the way I came with the carbine.

Yeah I say.

He looks at Darius and snorts, spits again. Goddam ridge runner he says. Come down from up on top and don' know nothen. Darius laughs.

What you want to go into town for, ridge runner? Okie says. He pokes the rifle barrel into my chest real sudden. It clunks against my ribs and hurts like a son of a bitch. I can hear Darius goen in my kit but I don' look.

Ain' nothen for you in town, boy Okie says. Best you go on back up the mountain and stay with the rest of the runners.

Just take the whole fucken thing Darius he says, ain' no use to go rooten through there. It don' stop Darius. Okie turns back to me.

You turn out your pockets he says and he taps me with the rifle again. We could do you he says. Kill you just as easy as killen that shoat and nobody to know any differ'nt about it. Who'd care what happens to a ridge runner like you anyhow.

I know I say. We're about fifteen hunnerd feet above the valley and I figure he is right.

You turn out your pockets and keep your mouth shut and you be all right Okie says. Darius is goen through my stuff still and I can hear the Colt clink against somethen. I hate to think of these two with it but there is nothen to do about it. I wish I had left the thing with Hunter.

My daddy's dead I say. I don' know why I say it.

Looky here Darius says and holds up the Barlow knife. He has got it open and the blade looks shiny even under the cloudy sky. He tests it against his hairy forearm. Sharp he says. Okie holds the rifle on me but he is looken off somewheres else, after where the pig went. I dig in after the money I got in my pockets.

Tree fell on him I say. When he was cutten it down.

Okie takes the six dollars from me, shoves it in his pants. I think about what a 30-30 could do to you this close up. I seen one take the whole hind end off a groundhog one time at about two hunnerd yards, just tore it off and threw the 'hog about ten feet. I hold out the arrowhead to him, turn out my pockets so's he can see they ain' nothen in them. He takes the arrowhead, holds it out from him with his left hand, squinten. He knows I ain' goen to give him any trouble.

Leave me some to get a pack of smokes down to the valley I say. And a bottle for my uncle.

Shoot Okie says. He tosses the arrowhead back over his shoulder. It hits the smooth steel rail and gives out a pretty sound, like a note on my daddy's old jew harp. The flint busts into about twenty pieces.

That was a pretty old arrowhead I say. I don' know how old it was but I want to say somethen.

Gimme his shoes Darius says.

He's standen and looken at my feet. His shoes look like bags tied with string or somethen. Mine ain' much but they are better than that, an old pair of sneakers that was my daddy's.

His shoes ain' about to fit you, clubfoot Okie says. Darius is bouncen up and down, still standen on a railroad tie. He's got my kit in his hand. He just looks at Okie and sticks his lip out. He is retarded some I see.

Get out your shoes Okie says. He seems like he is tired of the whole thing now. Just go on and get on out of them he says. He ain' even holden the rifle on me now.

I take my shoes off and hand them to Darius. He don' even try to put them on. He just stuffs them in the kit and laughs, sound like a dog barken. The roadbed is cold with the rain and the cinders stick to the soles of my feet, stain them black.

Darius goes to the edge of the right of way, looks off into the brush. Le's see can we get that pig now Okie he says. He goes off into the brush carryen my kit with him. After a minute I can' see him anymore, just hear him crashen around in there.

Okie looks me up and down and his eyes are still hard. The smell of him that close up is greasy, like somethen fat cooked on an open fire.

You go back on up he says. That's best for ridge runners, the top of the mountain.

I'm headed into town I say.

He looks mad at me and I think for a minute he may shoot me, but he don' even bring the gun around to bear. He looks at me some more, then heads on into the brush after Darius.

I wait a minute to see if they're comen back but they're both gone. No use tryen to follow them into the brush with no shoes. I start down the right of way again, on into the valley. The walken is easier without my kit. The rain has started up again, lighter this time. It don' feel like the kind of a rain that goes on for too long.

The cinders make my feet sore and black. I walk that way for a while, then change to walken on the ties. It is strange the small steps you have to take, but easier than stretchen to skip a tie every time. I get used to it.

*   *   *

When we find my daddy he's been dead for quite a while. The tree just caught him across the chest with one thick branch. He must of been on his way to dodge the fall when it caught him. His face looks surprised; his body don' look like anythen I ever seen before, all a different shape from what it was, crushed ribs and tore cloth, somethen terrible to look at. Hunter covers him with a good thick tarpaulin right after we jack the tree up off of him and I don' have a chance to look at him after that. We bury the tarpaulin along with him.

The loggen saw's down on the ground next to him. It didn' get caught by the tree at all, looks just like it had when he walked out with it. All the gas in it ain' gone so it must of stalled after he got hit. Hunter and me talk about it but can' never figure what it was about that old oak that made it fall the wrong way or why my daddy didn' figure how it was goen to come down. He must of made the cut wrong somehow and just not seen his mistake until it was too late.

* * *

Lot of folks lost everthen says the man who owns the drugstore. He is a heavy man wearen a white apron tied behind his back. Houses, stock, barns, the whole kitten caboodle down the river and on into Monroe County. He is talken to a skinny man in overalls who nods.

You betcha the drugstore man says. We awful lucky to be this high up. He is sweepen at a puddle of water near the door of his store, pushen the water out into the street. He wears glasses and the glass flashes as he moves his head in time with the broom. The bristles of the broom have soaked up a lot of the dirty water and he works like they are heavy.

The town is quiet, like it's a Sunday, and the streets are wet from the rain. When I walk in the store the men look at me. They see I got no shoes on.

Sucked the pilens right out from under the bridge the drugstore man says. Craziest thing you ever saw. Help you he says to me. I got no money so I don' say anythen back.

The Dodge dealership down to the river the skinny man says. You know, Sims'. Say the cars was floaten up near around the ceilen. Water came in so fast nobody had time to move nothen. Earth dam couple miles up let go and that was all she wrote.

Don' I know the drugstore man says. He sweeps some water past my feet, looks at me again. You need somethen he says.

I was looken for some smokes I say. Cigarettes.

We got them the drugstore man says. All kinds. What was you looken for?

Camels I say.

It's a bunch of miles down the mountain and I feel tired, sick. I want to sit down and have a smoke. I wish I had some money. My feet hurt.

Yo Carl the drugstore man says. You want to go in there back of the counter and get a pack of Camels for me.

Sure the skinny man says. He gets the cigarettes and tosses them to me. I catch them against my chest and the pack crushes a little.

I got no money I say.

The drugstore man stops sweepen a minute. Some of the water he just got out the door trickles back in. It's dirty river water, brown on the white tile floor.

Day like today I guess that's all right he says. He grins at me and I know how dirty I am. I know how I look. He figures I got wiped out by the flood.

My daddy's dead I say.

The drugstore owner shakes his head.

What a day Carl says behind the counter. He shakes his head too, snags himself a pack of smokes. What a day. I don' tell them that my daddy was dead before the rain even started.

That's hard son the drugstore man says. Awful goddam hard.

You got to wonder what the Lord is up to the skinny man says. Leave a boy 'thout a father.

I figure that is the nicest thing I ever heard. All I want to do right then is sit down and cry. I tear the wrap off the pack of cigarettes and the drugstore man hands me his lighter, a plastic Cricket. Coleman's Since 1942 it says on the side, the name of his drugstore. I turn the striken wheel with my thumb and the lighter catches, sends up a good strong flame the very first time.

* * *

I suck in the smoke and the third cigarette tastes just as good as the first. There is nothen like a butt that somebody else has rolled in a machine for you and that don' leave pieces of tobacco on your tongue.

I sit out near the end of the bridge that must of used to connected the two parts of the town across the river. It was an old steel bridge that sat up on stone pilens, and the drugstore man was right: the supports are clean gone and the span is down by the middle in the dark rushen river. Right near where I sit there's a sign that says Weight Limit 2 Tons.

I pull on the cigarette until it burns down near my fingers. I seen men that smoked so much they built up yellow callus on their thumb and pointer finger, could burn a smoke all the way down if they wanted to and never feel it at all. I can' do that and besides I got a whole pack yet to go. No use to be hard on myself. I flick the butt into the river and it is gone in the fast water almost even before I see it hit.

I have heard that in floods you will sometimes see animals and trees that got caught in the water goen downstream. I have not seen any by this time and figure they must all of been pushed down the river right at first when the water was highest. There probably won' be any again until the next time the river rises.

It is starten the hard rain again, not just the soft drizzle now, and I have to shield the fourth cigarette against the water to get it to light. The lighter catches the first try. I figure the cigarette will burn pretty well in the rain once

I manage to start it goen. I am wet again but this time it is not so pleasant as it was this mornen. This time it is just cold and nasty. I ain' sure what I will do. It is sure as hell I won' go back up the mountain.

After a while I may go up the river and look for the earth dam that let go and did all the damage. It must look pretty awful, busted open in the middle and oozen the river water over the lip of the hole, brown and thick with bottom mud. Not like the creeks up on the mountain but a real river and comen through just the way it wants with nothen to hold it back. Yessir, that would sure be somethen to see.